For Becky Sumner

1

KAY

THERE'S ALWAYS BEEN something missing inside of me. Well, maybe not always but for so long that it might as well have been forever. I can't remember the exact moment when the emptiness and longing seeped inside. To my surprise, my father's death hadn't deepened the hole. It was the same as it ever was. His passing only pushed the emptiness to the forefront of my thoughts. And suddenly I had to know everything about him and our past.

Dad always told me to stay out of the attic, claiming it was just a bunch of dusty old stuff I didn't need to bother myself with. I had always been curious, though, and as a child, I tried to sneak in a few times. He caught me every time. After the third time, he chose to punish me, and I stopped trying after that. Now that he was gone and no longer able to dole out consequences, I headed up to the attic to see what I would find.

Armed with a flashlight, I got up on my tippy toes and pulled the string to open the door and lowered the stairs. Ready for the climb, I tucked the flashlight in my back pocket, and headed up.

It was dark, and I could taste the dust in my mouth. Perhaps Dad had been telling me the truth all along.

At the top, I switched on the flashlight, illuminating the space. To my relief, there were no sounds of creepy crawlies—like pattering claws on hardwood or the scurrying of spiders. There was only silence. It was as if I'd stepped into another world where sound was devoid, along with the light, aside from the one I held in my hand.

The roof was sloped, and dozens of boxes were stacked along the walls. That was it—boring. No haunted dolls or old furniture with time-forgotten knickknacks. Just brown cardboard boxes stacked everywhere. Other than an earthquake making them tumble, I couldn't imagine what danger or secret would lead my father to be so adamant about me not exploring it.

Maybe there was something inside the boxes, something he didn't want me to know about. There were a lot of things he didn't want me to know about.

As a child with so many questions running through my head all day, every day, he shut most of them down. I learned not to ask questions and to be as obedient as possible.

It worked, for the most part.

I propped the flashlight on one stack of boxes and pulled down another. Maybe it would have been a better idea to bring up a lamp, but in the moment, my impatience got the better of me. I tore open the lid of the box. It was filled with textbooks. I pulled out the first one: *Psychology*. And the next, more psychology books. Nothing interesting. I knew my father had gone to college to study psychology. He had a practice and was a well-respected professional within the community. I pushed the box aside and went for the next. More books. Three boxes later, all I had found was more old textbooks from what I guessed were my father's graduate and undergraduate years. It wasn't until that fifth box that I hit the jackpot.

Photo albums.

I picked up the first, carefully flipping the lid. I gasped. It was a wedding album.

There was Dad, with a woman with blonde hair and blue eyes. She had a crooked smile, as if she wondered if she had just made a mistake. It was not the expression you'd expect from a woman on her wedding day.

On the next page, there were more pictures of the woman and my dad with what looked like friends, maybe family. There were tables and tables of them. Who was this woman? Based on the clothing, it was well before I would've been born. Had Dad been married before Mom?

Maybe it was a secret he kept guarded and didn't want me to know. Was he ashamed to have been a divorcée? Some people were funny about that, thinking divorce somehow put a stain on you. It was silly.

I didn't recognize anyone other than Dad in the next photo album. It was newer, and the woman smiling next to Dad was more familiar. Could it be my mother?

He'd never let me see photos of her, saying he was too heart-broken after her death. He explained she died during childbirth, giving life to me while hers was taken away. He said I was too young to understand and all I needed to know was that Mom was beautiful, loving, and kind.

As I continued flipping through the pages, I assumed the woman was my mother, and as the years progressed, a little girl appeared. A baby, a girl—was it me?

I had never seen photos of myself as a child. Dad said he didn't believe in keeping them, or so he had claimed. But it couldn't be me.

The woman was smiling and holding the baby close to her

chest. My mother had died during childbirth, so she couldn't have held me afterward, smiling and gazing down at me lovingly like that. My heart beat faster as I turned the pages, watching as the little girl grew. She had blonde hair and blue eyes, chubby cheeks, and little fingers.

She looked like me, but it wasn't me.

This little girl had a mole on her cheek and a button nose. Something inside of me stirred, and a memory connected, firing off in my brain.

My sister.

Dad was distraught when he told me she had died. It was sudden and unexpected.

My last memory of her was playing in our room. We were hiding under the covers, pretending there was a monster, and she told me we had to hide to survive. She had snuck in a flashlight, just like the one I had brought to the attic, and we read a book. She said if we were quiet, the monsters would go away.

The next morning, I woke up, and she was gone. Dad said there had been an accident, but there hadn't been a funeral or a memorial or any kind of service to mark her passing.

When I asked about her, Dad said I was too young to understand and that it was too heartbreaking to think about and forbid me from talking about her. It was his answer to everything. He'd always claim it was all too difficult to talk about.

In that moment, the memories of Sissy came flooding back as did her absence and my pleas to understand. "Daddy, what happened to Sissy? Where is she? Can I go see her?"

He had shut down my questions as fast as I could ask them. And again, I learned not to ask, and all these years later, I had nearly forgotten what Sissy looked like and so many of the memories had faded.

But I was beginning to think the morning I woke and

learned Sissy was gone was the moment the emptiness settled inside my soul and hadn't lifted all these years later.

The returned memories turned into more questions.

Where was my mother buried? Was she with Sissy? Perhaps it was time I found out for myself so I could visit their graves to say goodbye. Finally, I would be allowed to grieve like a normal person. Maybe it was the lack of closure with my mother and sister that kept the emptiness ever-present.

Dad would have wanted to be buried next to them, so I would have to find them anyway.

There was no time like the present, and I felt an urgency to find their graves and work on the plans for Dad's burial.

The medical examiner had promised the autopsy would be completed and his body released soon. The paramedics said it looked like he had a heart attack, but they couldn't be sure. You would think I'd be more curious as to his cause of death, but somehow his death freed me to find the answers to the questions I had been asking my whole life.

Determined, I remained in the cramped space seeking information about my early years. The boxes were all I had left, and I wanted to know everything.

In a frantic haze, I inspected every box only stopping when I had finished.

But after all the hours spent searching through boxes, instead of finding answers, I only unearthed more questions.

Why wasn't there a single photograph of me?

Where was my original birth certificate? And for that matter, where were the marriage certificates and the birth records? There was nothing official, just photographs, old textbooks, and a trophy with no name engraved on the base, presumably from Dad's younger years.

Where were the records of my mother and sister? Had they really existed? I knew they had because in my mind, I could still see Sissy under the covers next to me, giggling—a memory that never faded.

The most troubling part was not just the absence of any official records for my mother and sister but also the lack of any for me. Not even a photograph. A heaviness filled me as I realized if anyone tried to piece together my father or my life, there would be no trace of me.

2

MARTINA

As I LISTENED to Vincent talk about his winter getaway with his wife, Amanda, I could tell he was still in the throes of his love story despite the years they'd been together. Maybe that's what true love was. That deep, can't-get-enough-of-you love that lasted forever. It wasn't always physical, but it was still there— you knew they were your person, and you couldn't wait to see them after being apart. I could tell that was what it was like for Vincent and Amanda, and I couldn't help but wonder if that was what was happening to me.

Part of me knew it was silly to even think that way. We hadn't gone on a single date, and we couldn't—not for a while anyhow. Just friends, good friends. Whatever we called it didn't matter. I was falling madly in love with Charlie. Maybe it was because we were friends and hadn't let the physical stuff get in the way of our emotional connection that I had fallen so deeply for him. It was him, Charlie, I couldn't get enough of. Our conversations, his laugh, and the twinkle in his eyes when he greeted me.

He was a few weeks away from the coveted one-year chip. It was a huge accomplishment and, more selfishly, when he was technically cleared to start a romantic relationship. My heart skipped at the thought of what could happen next between Charlie and me. Did he feel the way I did?

Was I a total sap now?

My thoughts were interrupted when Hirsch entered the conference room, looking less than happy.

"Hi, Hirsch. Rough morning?" I asked.

He sighed. "It wasn't great."

"Oh?" Jayda asked from the other side of the table.

"Yeah, I just got news, and I'm not too happy about it."

What was it? At the end of our previous meeting, Hirsch had confirmed there was still funding for the Cold Case Squad through the year for us halftime consultants as well as half of Jayda and Ross's time. But something told me things were about to change once again.

He sat down. "Well, I'll just rip the Band-Aid off." He frowned. "The sheriff and I have been in discussions over the last six months, and unfortunately, we need to put together a task force to review all of Detective Leslie's homicide convictions over the last ten years."

Oh, that was bad news. No wonder he was looking so down. It had been devastating to learn that Detective Leslie had been working with members of organized crime. Not because she wanted to, but because they had threatened her son. She kept it quiet, still working with them. She said it was out of fear, but she should've known better, that she could've talked to someone. We could've helped her and ensured her safety.

Instead, she continued to lie, thwarting our investigation, helping the enemy. Now every case she'd ever worked was put into question. The news had spread like wildfire. The solved murder cases. The criminals she had put in prison. Those who had heard about the scandal were contacting lawyers to try to get their convictions overturned, and considering they were sitting in prison, they didn't have much else to do than fight to get out. The sheriff's department had a flurry of cases that had to be reviewed, and I was guessing that was going to take priority over solving cold cases.

"The sheriff's decided to divert all funds from the Cold Case Squad to reviewing and reworking Leslie's old cases to avoid lawsuits and the continued appeals pouring out of the prison system."

Hirsch's announcement sucked the air out of the room. I should've known better than to be so darn optimistic on a Monday morning, thinking about sugarplum fairies and true love—things that were just a fantasy or a hopeful dream compared to the harsh reality of this.

I said, "Sorry to hear it, Hirsch, but I understand. The sheriff has a lot of pressure on him right now."

"He does. But just because I agree with him doesn't mean I have to like it."

"I get it."

"The official word is any cases that are currently open can be worked and then wrapped up. But then we're supposed to thank Martina and Vincent for their time, as the contracts will be ended. Jayda and Ross, you're free to go back to homicide full-time until you're assigned some of Leslie's cases." Hirsch frowned at the message.

My heart was heavy.

That was it.

It was over.

It wasn't the first time Vincent and I had been told, "thanks, bye," but it stung all the same. We'd gotten too comfortable knowing there was funding. But that could change at a moment's notice, which was why when Sheriff Baldwin wrote our contracts they were open-ended, no guarantee of duration.

It wasn't the end of the world, but it was a little sad. The past few years showed us that no matter what, Hirsch, Jayda, Ross, and all the old Cold Case Squad members, with the exception of Detective Leslie, of course, would be in our lives. And I had plenty of work to do at my firm, Drakos Monroe Security & Investigations. "Who will be working on Leslie's old cases?"

"Sheriff Baldwin is still deciding who to put on it. It's got to be somebody with a squeaky-clean record. It could be Jayda or Ross, since you're two of our strongest detectives. But we also need you solving fresh cases," Hirsch explained.

"Understood, boss," Jayda responded.

"Guess that means we're free to go?" Vincent asked.

Considering we had just wrapped up our last case, it was a valid question. "You are."

Vincent eyed me, as if hoping there was a way to make it stop. I said, "Our cases at Drakos Monroe have had us cross paths on more than one occasion. So, you'll never really get rid of us."

With the very hint of a smile, Hirsch said, "I wouldn't have it any other way."

Vincent and I chatted with Hirsch and Jayda and Ross for about an hour, drinking coffee and catching up after the 4th of July holiday. They were a great team, like a family, but considering we were no longer working for CoCo County, Vincent and I had to head back to Drakos Monroe to finish up the day and go home to our families.

With Zoey off at college during most of the year, the house was quieter. The only sounds were Barney's barking, pattering on the floors, running, and fetching after balls and toys, letting everybody know that he was still the boss of all the stuffed frogs. Of course, a lot of my down time was spent with Mom and Ted and Darren and Izzy, who seemed to be doing really well. Izzy just got her three-month chip for sobriety, and Darren had his five-month. Change wasn't always for the worse.

And of course, my new friend and I spent a lot of time together, talking about life, love, and books. Charlie had just finished the first draft of his novel and sent it off to his publisher. I couldn't wait to celebrate with him, and a few other friends, of course. With the Cold Case Squad disbanded once again, my days would free up even more, but I didn't think for a second that meant life would get boring. Because in the past, the moment I did, my world was turned up on its head once again. The only question was, what would come next?

3

KAY

THE FUNERAL DIRECTOR, a man is in his late fifties, had a dignified yet warm presence. His hair, graying at the temples, was carefully combed over. His face, marked with gentle lines, spoke of years of experience in a grim profession. Dressed in a well-tailored suit, he exuded an air of respectability. The office around him reflected his role.

The furniture was beige, but the décor was elegant, with a blend of professional and comforting elements. He sat behind a big desk, which held a few neatly arranged papers and a desktop computer. On the walls, there were certificates of his professional qualifications, along with watercolors in hues of blues and greens. He said, "I'm glad to hear you're feeling better and are able to start planning your father's memorial."

"Yes, thank you. The medical examiner hasn't released his body yet, and I don't want to have the memorial before it is. But I figured we could start on the memorial stone since I recall you saying it could take a while. Also, I'd like to ensure he'll have a spot next to my mother and sister's graves," I replied. "The only problem is I'm not sure where they are."

I had gone on the internet and did a search, trying to find where they might be buried, but I came up empty-handed.

"Well, we should be able to find them, no problem. Do you have their names and social security numbers?"

I scrunched up my face and shook my head. "No, I have my mother's name, but I don't have their social security numbers or my sister's first name. I only remember calling her Sissy. I went through all my dad's records in the attic and couldn't find any for my mother and sister, just Dad's."

The man cocked his head, as if it was a peculiar situation, and it was. Where were the records of my mother and sister? I had tried to unlock Dad's computer, assuming all the records had to be somewhere, and it seemed like a logical place. But I wasn't able to guess his password.

"We'll do everything we can with the names. If we can't find them, we might have to enlist the help of an investigator," he said. "It would be helpful to know where they've lived and maybe more about your extended family."

All the things I didn't know. Although I did recall moving around as a child, I was far too young to understand what our address was or the ZIP code. I just knew Dad was a psychiatrist. Because he was my only known relative, he had been my whole world after Sissy was gone.

"I'm not sure how much help that'll be. I have Dad's birth certificate, social security number, and employer's information, but I didn't find anything official like addresses or old mail. Just our current home that we've lived at since I was ten years old, so it's been about fifteen years, and they both died before then," I explained.

"That would be a good start. How long ago did your mother and sister pass?"

"My mother died during childbirth, so twenty-five years ago. And my sister..." My voice trailed off, trying to remember exactly when she died. I think I was six, so that meant Sissy was seven or eight. Why couldn't I remember for sure?

Sissy liked to show me the ropes, like how to hide from the monsters and how to sneak cookies without Dad noticing. She didn't talk much, but when she did, she'd tell me all her discoveries. "I'm not entirely sure. I was six when she passed, so she must've died nineteen years ago. She was a year or two older than me."

"That's not a lot to go on, I'm afraid, but I'll see what I can do."

"I'd appreciate it. I'm sure Dad would want to be laid to rest beside them, and I'd like to visit their graves, too. Dad was against us ever visiting, so I've never been."

The man gave me a puzzled look. "I'll look into it. I can call around and see if anybody may know where the grave markers are. If I can't find their locations, I'll give you a call."

"Thank you."

"Have you thought about what kind of service you'd like to have?" he asked.

"I'm not sure. Nothing too big. And it should be on a weekend, so people won't have to take time off work. Maybe more like a celebration of life than a funeral."

"Oh, that would be lovely. Do you know how many people may attend?"

I didn't. Dad often talked about colleagues and friends, but he never brought them to the house. In hindsight, it was strange that I never met any of them, with the exception of a few men he said were colleagues. I only knew their first names like Tim, Ted, Mike, or Mark—common names. Outside of contacting his employer and asking who his friends and colleagues were, I had no idea how to reach those who may want to pay their respects.

"I'm not sure. I'll have to reach out to his practice to see how many people he was close with."

"You don't have any other family?"

"No. Dad was an only child, and so was my mother. Both of their parents have passed."

"All right. I recommend you reach out to your father's workplace. It sounds like it might be a small service. Just let me know the numbers, and we'll start working on a plan and a quote for the service."

I thanked him and wondered what he would find. He was a funeral director and must have ways to find where people were buried that weren't obvious to me or the internet.

As I walked out of the funeral home, an unsettling thought struck me. I didn't know who my father's friends were. He had no family and no records of his wife or children.

It was all a little odd.

In my apartment, I had all the records from my jobs, from school. Maybe he just wasn't someone who kept things around or had digitized them years earlier. He did always like to have the house spic and span. If the funeral director couldn't find some answers, I wasn't sure what I would do.

OVER THE WELL-WORN BREAKFAST TABLE, I sipped on orange juice while I explained my visit to the funeral home the day before to my roommate Becky. Becky and her family were originally from the Bay Area, but the two of us hadn't met until our first year in the dorms at Saint Mary's College. She was one of my very best friends and like a sister from another mister. She took the last bite of crumpet and said, "That does seem a little strange. No records of your mom or your sister? I didn't even know you had a sister."

Because Dad had never wanted to speak of them, and the memories of Sissy were so faint, I didn't usually tell people because it was too complicated to explain. "I do. I was really young when she passed, but I still have these fuzzy memories of her."

Before I could explain further, my phone rang. "Do you mind if I grab this? It's the funeral director."

"Of course, go ahead."

Phone up to my ear, I said, "Hello."

"Miss Griffin, I have some bad news. I wasn't able to find the location of your mother and sister's graves. Is there any other information you can give me that would help me identify them?"

"I only have photographs," I said staring out at our cheerful living space. There were photographs of Becky and my college pals and oils Becky had painted. Despite her degree in business, she was a talented artist on top of being a bombshell reminiscent of a young Sophia Loren who loved to make fudge and dance in the rain.

"Well, I'm afraid that's not going to help."

"Do you have any suggestions of what I should do?"

"It could get kind of expensive, but you could talk to a private investigator. They might be able to find the details of your dad's life, which could help us figure out your mother's and sister's details and their current location."

"Oh, okay," I said, feeling overwhelmed.

"Has the medical examiner released your father's remains?"

"Not yet. I'll call when we're ready to schedule the service."

"Okay, just let me know. Have a nice day, Miss Griffin."

After thanking him, I ended the call and placed my phone back atop the table.

Becky looked at me with concern. "What was that about?"

"He can't find where my mom and sister are buried, or any death records."

"That's strange. What did he say you should do?"

"Hire a private investigator."

"Well, that's not going to be cheap."

"No, but I know where Dad kept his stash." Dad didn't believe in traditional banking outside of one account to pay the mortgage and utilities. He said banks couldn't be trusted and had his life savings, in cash, inside the house. And I knew where it was, thanks to my snooping. "There's some cash my dad left at the house. I could use it."

I thought Dad would think it would be a worthwhile expenditure to have him placed near his beloved wife and daughter.

Becky said, "Oh yeah, that's right. Your dad was one of those anti-banking folks."

Becky had told me she thought Dad was an odd duck but nice enough. At first, I had defended him, but in hindsight and with the newfound information from the attic, I would have to agree with her.

"Yeah, well, I guess I have to find a private investigator now."

"I can help you with finding a PI, with the memorial. Anything you need," Becky offered kindly.

Despite my lack of familial connections, at least I had my friends. A strange feeling washed over me, and I felt like I had no real history. The funeral director had given me a good idea, though. Maybe a private investigator could answer all the questions I had. Maybe, at last, I would learn the truth and, at last, become whole.

4

MARTINA

It had been two days since we received the news we would no longer be working with Hirsch and the team at CoCo County. From my experience, it didn't necessarily mean a permanent separation, but maybe only a brief hiatus. It was a change, but as I sat in my office at Drakos Monroe, it seemed as if nothing had changed at all. I found myself back at my desk, entrenched in the daily routine. But maybe it was time for a change. My office needed to be tidied, and I could use some more recent photos of Zoey. I picked up the framed picture on my desk and admired the vision of Zoey with a giant smile showing off her missing front teeth. My bookshelves could use a dusting and a clean out. Spring cleaning. That was what I needed to do.

A notification popped up on my screen.

Cleaning would have to wait.

Clutching my mug, I made my way toward the conference room where Vincent was scheduled to meet a new client. Upon arrival, I noticed the room was empty and the only items inside were the shiny new oval table with four black leather chairs tucked into it. A whiteboard on the wall along with a few photographs, one of the Golden Gate Bridge at sunset and one of the ocean with waves crashing against a sandy beach.

Vincent must be either greeting the clients at the front desk or running a tad late. From the brief notes Vincent had provided, the case seemed straightforward. A young woman was seeking information about where some of her relatives were buried following her father's death.

If it were as simple as it sounded, all we needed to do was look up the death records and, at most, contact the hospitals where they were last seen. Checking with local funeral homes to ascertain where they had been buried would likely wrap it up. It seemed like an open-and-shut case, potentially just a day's worth of work.

As I glanced up, I saw Vincent, his face beaming, escorting two young women toward the conference room. Standing up, I greeted them with a smile. It was part of my role as the owner to ensure we projected a warm and caring image to our clients and to meet each of them during their first visit.

Vincent introduced me. "This is one of our owners, Martina Monroe. Martina, this is Kay Griffin and her friend Becky Sumner. Becky's here for moral support."

"It's nice to meet both of you," I said, extending handshakes before inviting them to take a seat at the conference table.

Vincent, taking his seat, explained, "Martina sits in on all new client meetings to assess how many resources we may need to work on your case."

They were younger than most of our clients. The women looked noticeably nervous, especially Kay. Maybe the passing of her father had ruffled her.

Vincent said, "Why don't you tell us about what brought you in today?"

"Well, my father died five days ago," she replied, as she placed her hands in her lap.

"I'm so sorry for your loss. How did he pass, if you don't mind me asking?" Considering the fact she was looking for family members, I wondered if there were unusual circumstances around his death.

"Thank you. We're not exactly sure. I was coming over for dinner and found him on the kitchen floor unconscious. I called 911 right away, but he was pronounced dead on the scene. The medical examiner still hasn't finished the autopsy yet."

A suspicious death? "I'm guessing that could bring up a lot of feelings about family and loss."

"Yes. It's why I'm here. He didn't have a will, at least not one that I know of. I don't know what he would have wanted as far as burial, but I figured he'd want to be buried next to my mother and my sister. They both passed when I was very young —my mother during childbirth with me, and my sister when I was six. But I'm not sure where their graves are, and the funeral home can't find their location either."

The young woman was attempting to reunite her family in death. It was a sweet and loving gesture. Her father must have meant a great deal to her. But how could she have not known where her mother and sister were buried?

"Do you recall where your father, mother, and sister were living when they passed?" I asked.

"My father told me I was born in Portland, Oregon, and my mother died there too. As for my sister's death, I'm not sure. I assumed we were in California. I was only six at the time, and I only have faint memories of where we lived then. We moved around a lot when I was a kid, but I think we've always been in California."

"That's really helpful. Did you bring the paperwork you told me about on the phone?" Vincent asked.

Kay nodded. "Yes, I brought my dad's birth certificate and a few bills, but it's really the only official records I found."

"What about records of your mother and sister? Did you find their birth certificates, death certificates, marriage certificates? Anything like that?" I probed further.

Kay lowered her eyes. "No, I couldn't find anything other than photographs."

That was strange. You would think a man of Kay's father's age would have a whole slew of records—marriage, birth, death, tax. "What were your mother and sister's names?"

"My mother's name was Giselle and my sister…I'm not totally sure. I used to call her Sissy. And Dad wouldn't speak of her. He was too distraught after her death to talk about her."

That was more than a little strange. "But he was able to tell you your mother's name. Did he talk about her?"

"He didn't talk about her much, or at all. Dad always said it was best to leave the past behind you and to keep focused on what lay ahead. But her name is on my birth certificate."

"Did you bring your birth certificate?" I asked.

Kay looked panicked. "Oh, no. Just the documents I found at my father's house. Should I bring mine?"

"It's not critical right now. The other materials you brought should help. We'll take a look and see what we can find. If we need your birth certificate, we'll let you know," I assured her.

"I appreciate it."

"I'm guessing this is something you'd like to have done right away, considering that you want to put together a memorial for your father?"

"Yes."

"Have you already started with the funeral preparations?" I asked.

Kay furrowed her brow. "I want to, but I am having a difficult time deciding who to invite. I called his workplace and asked who his friends were, who I may need to invite to the memorial, and all they told me was to send over the details when they are available. They weren't sure of anybody he was particularly close to."

"How long had he worked there?"

"Fifteen years. As long as I can remember."

Something told me there was more to Kay's father than she realized. "And what did he do for work?" I asked.

"He was a psychiatrist."

"And do you have all the details for his practice in there?" I asked, pointing to the paperwork she brought.

"Yes."

"How about tax records? Did you find those?"

"No. I'm assuming they're on his computer, but I wasn't able to crack his password."

"That's fine. We should have enough information to find the location of your mother and sister's grave markers."

"Thank you so much," she said, her voice tinged with relief.

As much as I tried to assure her that finding what she was seeking would be no issue, the details didn't quite add up.

The funeral director should've been able to find the grave markers and their death certificates but hadn't. Was it because she didn't know her sister's name? Even so, she knew her mother's name, so it should have been easy to find. A sense of unease was stirring within me, and I took a deep breath, bracing for what we may find.

5

MARTINA

Vincent had agreed to do the initial background check on Ansel Griffin, which left me some time to start cleaning up my office. Rolling my chair back, I stood up and decided to tackle the easiest task first—wiping down my whiteboard. The board, filled with random notes and messages from people stopping by when I wasn't around, looked like a jumble of chaos. Chaos cluttered my mind, and I wanted to be clear-headed. Propping myself up, I picked up the eraser and wiped down the whiteboard. Thirty seconds later, it was done. I sighed and gazed over at my desk with its piles of papers and thought, *I guess there's no time like the present.*

Before I could continue my task, from my periphery, I spotted Vincent heading my way. His face was flushed, and he appeared to be in a rush.

Our eyes met. "What's up?" I asked.

"Found some interesting things, boss."

Something interesting enough to run over to my office? "Like what?"

"Shall we grab a room, or do you want to do this in here?"

The conference rooms were used for bigger cases. Whatever

Vincent had found in what should have been a simple background check and location of grave markers may not be as straightforward as we'd hoped.

There was something very strange about Kay Griffin's story concerning her father and her family. No records existed, except for photographs. I had a feeling about this one, but I liked to be wrong every once in a while. But the way Kay described her father, and his reluctance to speak of her mother or her sister, being too heartbroken to discuss the past... it didn't quite pass the smell test. My initial thoughts on Ansel Griffin were that he was hiding something, and maybe Vincent had discovered what that was.

"Here should be fine. Come on in."

Vincent entered and took one of the two chairs in front of my desk as I shut the door. "I have a clean whiteboard, so I'm ready for whatever you have."

"We'll see about that."

"I'm all ears, Vincent."

He leaned back and placed his arms across his chest. "First off, I did a standard background check on Ansel Griffin based on his birth certificate and social security number. I found his current address, property and employment records. Pretty standard stuff."

"Did you find the grave sites for his wife and daughter?" It was the job. Surely, he looked.

"Not yet..." he said, leaving a lingering question.

Surely he had found more. His theatrics were rearing their cheery head, I could feel it. "I'm guessing you have more information. Perhaps there are things you *didn't* find?"

"Ah ha!" he said, with a gleam in his eyes. "That's why you're the boss! Well, for starters, things I expected to find like a marriage license or his name listed as the father on a birth certification do not exist. Ansel Griffin has never been married or had children—at least not officially."

"That's odd, considering we've met his daughter, Kay."

Vincent pursed his lips and nodded. "It is, isn't it?"

"What else did you find?"

"You know me too well," Vincent replied with a hint of pride. "So, all this was really weird, right? So, I looked at the records a little closer and you know what's really strange?"

"No, what?"

"His, Ansel Griffin's, records only go back fifteen years. Before that..."

Well, well, well. "He didn't exist?"

"Oh no, he did. He was in fact born sixty-five years ago in Omaha, Nebraska."

"But?"

"But he also died sixty-four years and three hundred days ago."

An identity stolen from a deceased infant.

Ansel Griffin was not Ansel Griffin. I knew there was something off about the daughter's recollections. "So, everything Ansel, or whoever he was, told his daughter could be untruthful."

"That's where my mind went. On a hunch, I called Ansel Griffin's employer. You know, where his daughter says he's a psychiatrist? Well, turns out he's not a psychiatrist at all. He's a file clerk at the medical practice."

Why would he lie to his daughter about his profession? And his identity? "Did you ask his employer about his overall demeanor? If he had friends?"

"Well, the overall vibe is that he was kind of strange and mostly kept to himself."

My mind drifted back to Kay's statement about calling her

father's practice and being told to send the memorial notification but was unsure if he had any close friends.

"What do you think, boss?" Vincent asked while I tried to put the pieces of the Ansel Griffin puzzle together.

"He told his daughter he was a psychiatrist but was actually a file clerk. The fact he wouldn't speak of his wife and daughter who supposedly died is weird. He must be running from something. But what?"

We needed to bring in Kay to determine how far she wanted us to dig into her father's life. Her life. Learning her father had been, likely, lying to her for her entire life could be quite upsetting. But then, another idea struck me. Before we went back to her, we had friends who might be able to help us learn the truth about Ansel Griffin. "He lived in CoCo County, and his body is at the office of the medical examiner. Let's put in a call to Dr. Scribner and explain what we found. She and her team should be able to help us identify him."

"Fingerprints are easy."

Exactly.

"And if fingerprints are a no go, there's always DNA."

It was our best chance for learning the true identity of Ansel Griffin. If we could learn who he really was, we could find his wife and daughter's graves. Another thought popped into my head. "We should request Kay's birth certificate. Find out how she fits in with whoever this Ansel guy was."

Vincent's blue eyes lit up. "You call Dr. Scribner. I'll call Kay. Deal?"

With a satisfied grin, I said, "Deal."

It was good to be back in the game.

6

MARTINA

Vincent hurried off, and I picked up the receiver on my desk phone and called Dr. Scribner's office. My body practically tingled with anticipation. I knew we wouldn't be away from our pals in CoCo County for long. "Office of the Medical Examiner, how can I help you?"

"Dr. Scribner please."

"Who may I ask is calling?"

"Martina Monroe."

"Please hold."

With a pen in hand, I tapped the end on my desk until I heard my old friend's voice. "Hey, Martina. How are you doing? Just heard about the Cold Case Squad funding. Sorry to hear it."

"It's becoming par for the course."

"Yeah, budgets are all over the place, especially after what happened to Detective Leslie. That's hard."

"It is."

"So, how can I help you? I'm guessing you need something?"

Dr. Scribner was one of the most intelligent and delightful medical examiners I had ever worked with. Although there were a few others, she was sharp and always willing to lend a hand. In some ways, I thought of her as a mature version of my daughter, Zoey. Dr. Scribner wore sparkly red glasses and had a flair about her despite her grim occupation.

Zoey had always been fascinated by criminal investigations and loved all things sparkly. As much as I had wondered if she might go into criminal law, she seemed pretty set on becoming a veterinarian. I couldn't believe she had already completed her first year of college and was home, although busy with her friends, also home after their first year away for college. It was good to have her at home, but so many things had changed, and I was filled with anticipation for what was to come.

"You know me too well. Yes, I was hoping to get some help but also help you. I have a client whose father passed away recently. She was trying to find the grave markers of some family members to have them laid to rest together but was unable to locate them. So, we did a background check on her father and came up with some interesting findings. Long story short, we don't think he's who he says he is. We ran a background check and according to his name and social security number, the person with the name he goes by died when he was an infant."

"Is he someone who's on my table?" Dr. Scribner asked.

"He died five days ago. The daughter says his body is with you now and that the autopsy hasn't happened yet."

"He should be here. What's his name?" Dr. Scribner asked.

"He would've come in under the name Ansel Griffin."

Clicking of keys emanated from the speaker, followed by, "Oh yes, I have his autopsy scheduled for tomorrow. I'll have them run fingerprints right away. We do like to confirm the identities of our bodies. I'll call you as soon as the autopsy is complete."

"I would appreciate it."

"No problem. How are things with you? How is Zoey?"

"She's great. Home from school, lighting up the Bay Area."

"How does she like Davis?"

"She loves it."

It was true, and I worried she'd never want to move home, other than for summer break. After undergraduate years, she would be off to veterinary school and then she'd be on her own for the rest of her life. My baby girl was an adult, but she'd always be my girl.

"Great to hear. Tell her I said hello."

"Will do."

"All right, good talking to you, Martina. I'll give you a call as soon as I get the fingerprints run."

"Thank you." I hung up the receiver and spotted Vincent through the window in my office and waved him in.

"Well?" Vincent asked.

"The autopsy is scheduled for tomorrow. She'll call me after they run his fingerprints."

"What if he's not in the system?"

It was a good question. "Dental records. DNA."

"And if forensics don't tell us anything?"

A full-blown deep dive to unravel his past. Or we let it go. "It depends. Did you get a hold of Kay?"

"Yes, she's agreed to drop off her birth certificate."

"What have you told her?"

"Just that we were having some trouble finding records and that hers may be useful."

"Maybe we should reinterview her as well. Now that we know her father lied to her, we can probe her for more details."

Vincent smiled. "She'll be in tomorrow at one o'clock."

Perfect. Hopefully we'd glean more about her childhood and growing up with her father. We would have to do a full background check on Kay as well. This case could be a lot more complicated than we had anticipated, not to mention we may uncover things that could shatter Kay's memories of her father and her family.

7

KAY

MARTINA SEEMED NICE, and so did Vincent. Both appeared to genuinely care, but I couldn't shake the feeling they were withholding something. What was it they weren't telling me? When Vincent had called earlier, he hadn't explained why he needed my birth certificate or why they hadn't found anything useful about my father, or something that could lead to the location of my mother and sister's graves. Now, sitting across from them, I had a feeling I was about to find out why.

The conference room they had chosen seemed to have been designed to be uplifting, with its images of the ocean waves crashing against the Golden Gate Bridge and the walls were painted in a soft, warm eggshell. Handing my birth certificate and social security number to Vincent, I said, "There they are. If you need any more information about my life, I'm an open book."

Vincent said, "We're hoping this will help answer some questions and lead us to where your mother and sister are buried."

Martina gave him a side-eyed glance, a clear indication that he wasn't telling me everything.

I pressed on. "May I ask what you've found so far, and how you think it will help?"

I wished Becky were there, but she had to work. Meanwhile, I was still on bereavement leave from the law office where I worked as a communications manager.

Martina said, "We did find some surprising information about your father. We've also been in touch with the medical examiner. She's performing the autopsy today and promised to call us once it's done."

That was surprising. I hadn't realized medical examiners disclosed such information so readily. "Oh, good. That'll be helpful," I said, though I wasn't entirely convinced it answered my question.

Vincent said, "When you hired us, you asked us to find the graves of your mother and sister. As you suspected, it's difficult because there's little to no record of them, or even of your father. We have reason to believe that Ansel Griffin wasn't his real name."

I leaned back in my chair, instinctively distancing myself from these people. Their words were unsettling. He wasn't Ansel Griffin? Of course, he was Ansel Griffin. "I don't understand," I murmured, confused.

Martina's amber eyes conveyed a mixture of warmth and seriousness. "We did a background check on your father. We checked his birth records, the name on his birth certificate, and the associated social security number. It turns out it was for a baby boy born in Omaha, Nebraska. But that baby died a few days after birth. You see, when someone wants to adopt a new identity, it's common to use the birth certificate of a deceased infant. It's harder these days, but before everything was electronic, a person could create a whole new life based on these documents."

I shook my head, struggling to grasp the revelation. "If my

father isn't Ansel Griffin, then who is he?" The thought that my father might have been lying to me all those years was overwhelming. "So, if my father had been living under this Ansel Griffin identity for so long, why couldn't you find records of my mother and sister too?"

"Well," Vincent chimed in, "we didn't find any records for your father before fifteen years ago. Based on what you've told us, your mother and sister would've already been deceased by then. It's possible they're connected to him through a different identity, perhaps his birth name. We're hoping the medical examiner can help us determine his true identity. This, in turn, might lead us to your mother and sister, if that's still what you want."

I sat back, trying to process this bombshell. Was this why we moved around so much before settling in Pleasant Hill? Was this why he never spoke of the past? Why he made me stay clear of the attic and his old things? He had started over, but why? And why hadn't he told me about it?

Vincent said, "Kay, I know this is a lot. Can I get you anything? A beverage? Tea, coffee, water?"

"No," I said, still reeling. "Why would someone do that?"

Martina and Vincent looked at each other again. Martina said, "There are a number of reasons why someone might want to start fresh. Maybe they faced a tragedy and didn't want to be found. Or perhaps they witnessed a crime, gave evidence, and decided to change their identity." She paused, then added, "But we doubt he was in witness protection, because if he had been he would've been given a new identity, not have used a deceased person's. Maybe he was running from something—either the law or someone was after him for any number of reasons."

What had my father been running from? This new information about him made small tidbits of his life flash through my mind.

He rarely mentioned friends, and when he did, it was first names only. I had never visited his place of work, only heard about it from him. We supposedly didn't have any family, and he insisted we never talk about the past. As I pondered this, I could feel Vincent and Martina's eyes on me, as though they expected me to respond.

"One of the reasons we brought you here is to ask if you want us to continue investigating," Vincent said. "We can uncover the true identity of your father and the reason behind the new life he created for himself and for you. But we need to know if that's what you really want."

Did I want the truth? Even if it revealed something terrible? "I do. I want to know, especially if it helps me find my mom and my sister." My memories of my mother were nonexistent, but the images of my sister stuck with me. My father had told me she was gone, but he had lied about his identity. Could he have lied about my mother and sister too?

"No problem, we'll continue our investigation," Martina reassured me. "But we also need to ask about your childhood. It could help us piece together the details of your family and your life."

Details of my childhood. There were things I had kept locked away. Did it matter if I shared them now? It wasn't like Dad could punish me from the beyond. "What do you want to know?"

"What's your earliest memory of your father? Of your sister?" Vincent asked.

Most of my memories were of playing with Sissy in our room. Everything before that seemed blank. "It's been so long... I think I was five or six. Most of my memories are with Sissy and me, playing together."

"And your father—did he ever remarry or have girlfriends? Did friends visit the house?" Martina asked.

"No, he never dated that I knew of. He had a few friends, but they never stayed long, and I never knew their last names."

"Was there anything unusual about your childhood, or something that seemed out of place? You mentioned moving around a lot. Do you remember why?" Martina asked.

"I don't know why we moved so much, and I don't remember much about the different cities we lived in. We didn't go out much. I was homeschooled until we settled in Pleasant Hill. My father said it was best not to make too many new attachments until we found our permanent home." As I said the words, it did seem strange. All of it did.

Martina's expression was warm, but something in her face betrayed her thoughts. What I was sharing was, indeed, odd. I hadn't really considered it until now, but my childhood was unusual. I didn't recall having friends until we settled in Pleasant Hill when I was ten. Perhaps that was why losing Sissy hit me so hard. She wasn't just my sister; she was my only friend. It was so long ago that I guessed I had blocked out that part.

But I was never totally lonely. I read a lot of books, and Dad was there to keep me company.

"Your dad homeschooled you, but he was a psychiatrist?" Martina asked.

I nodded. "He only worked part-time. I guess I never really put the pieces together until now. Maybe that's why we hadn't settled. Perhaps he couldn't find full-time work. I just don't know." It was so confusing. Nothing made sense.

Martina said, "We also discovered that although your father worked at Delta Medical Practice, he was not a psychiatrist. He was a file clerk."

I felt like the air had been knocked out of me.

Nothing he told me was true.

"Are you sure?" I asked, immediately realizing how pointless the question was. Of course, they were sure.

"Is there someone we can call for you? Your friend Becky? This isn't a time to be alone," Vincent suggested gently.

"She's actually my roommate, so I'll talk to her when she gets home."

"Are you sure? We can give you a ride home, too, if you'd like. This is a lot to take in," Martina offered.

My mind was frozen from all the information, too much to process. "I'll be okay. Thank you though. Do you have any other questions for me? Something that might help you find the truth?" I tried to retain my composure.

"Understanding where you'd been living before your father's most current address would be helpful. Did you always live in California? I believe you mentioned that the first time we spoke," Vincent asked.

I shook my head. "I remember long drives and lots of trees, the coast, forests... I just assumed it was all California." But now, I wasn't so sure.

"Was your father warm and loving, or was he strict?" Martina asked.

"He was strict in some ways, yes. He didn't like it if I disobeyed him. He didn't like me asking about the past, about Mom or Sissy. He said it was too sad. I guess I learned not to ask a lot of questions."

A quiet fell over the room with my statement.

In that moment, I realized I knew nothing about my past. I didn't know where I had lived. I hadn't had any friends or family other than Dad for the first ten years, except for Sissy. It was unnatural.

Once I moved into the dorms at college, I met so many friends who talked about their childhoods and had families who would visit. Becky had photo albums of her entire family from the time she was born and even had childhood friends visit her while we lived on campus together. I didn't have any of that. Dad visited but I had no photos to share as a young child. Just pictures of friends from high school and junior high. It was like before then I didn't exist. It was a terrible realization that all the things about my childhood and family before the age of ten were what my father had told me. And I feared the stories were riddled with lies.

8

MARTINA

My heart went out to Kay. I could only imagine the tumultuous feelings she must be experiencing, finding out that someone she trusted, someone who had been her entire world until she was ten years old, had been lying to her for her entire life.

We would need to keep in touch with Kay throughout the investigation. Not only to follow up on leads but also to ensure that she was mentally okay and had the proper support. Kay seemed to have good friends, but no family. With such startling revelations, she was going to need all the support she could get. I sincerely hoped we could find the answers she needed and it would allow her to make sense of what we'd told her.

Vincent offered to escort Kay back to the lobby. We shook hands, and I told her earnestly, "Call me if you need anything." I wanted her to know that I meant it—whether she needed resources, the name of a good counselor, anything at all. Her father, the very person who should have been her real support, had failed her.

There was something in her answers, however, that made me question if she was telling us everything. Was it a newfound sense of distrust for others, stemming from her father's deceit? It wouldn't be uncommon. Discovering a trusted person's lies often leads to questioning the motives of others as well.

Back in my office, I picked up my laptop and coffee cup, contemplating the day's events. The boring task of tidying up, which I had embarked on earlier, now seemed trivial. Yet, a clean desk often meant a clear mind. As I sifted through the stack of papers—memos, vacation requests, invoices, the usual administrative duties I least enjoyed as part-owner of the firm—Vincent knocked on my door.

"I spoke with Kay," he said, stepping into my office.

"How did she seem when you said goodbye?"

"She seemed shook up, but there's something else too. Like she was surprised, but not shocked to the core. Maybe she had begun to have her own suspicions?"

"Maybe, but did you get the feeling that she wasn't telling us everything too?"

"Perhaps. Maybe not intentionally."

"It's possible. Will you be able to do the background check on Kay?"

Nodding, he said, "I'll start with checking birth records to see if Kay is who she thinks she is."

"Smart." We both knew this investigation could reveal another bombshell for Kay—that she might not be Kay Griffin. At twenty-five, she was an adult but still young and vulnerable.

"No word from Dr. Scribner about the autopsy?"

"Not yet. But it's scheduled for today. We may not hear anything until tomorrow."

Vincent lingered in the doorway. "Do you think we have enough resources? Just you and me on this one?"

"For now, yes." I paused and wondered why he thought that. "Do you already have theories?"

"Not quite. But I feel like there's something really off here."

I nodded in agreement. "Once we learn his true identity, we'll start digging deeper. We'll want to find any relatives, if he has any, and of course learn more about Kay. And with what we've discovered so far, it'll be interesting to learn his cause and manner of death."

"Do you think he was murdered?"

It had crossed my mind. The way Kay described the events leading to the discovery of her father's body left a lot to interpretation. He could have died of natural causes, or he could have been murdered in a way that mimicked natural causes, like being injected with a drug that induced a heart attack. At 65, it wasn't improbable for a heart attack, but we knew so little about his health, lifestyle, or genetics—and his true identity. "If he was murdered, Dr. Scribner will tell us."

"At this point, I wouldn't be surprised," Vincent said. "It could be that whatever or whoever he was hiding from finally found him."

That possibility could make this case more complex. "Let's try not to speculate too much or put that energy out into the universe," I cautioned.

Vincent chuckled. "Been a while since we've had a whopper of a case, don't you think?"

I froze and then shook my head. "Now you're going to jinx it, Vincent."

"You don't believe in that kind of stuff, do you?"

Not really, but I wasn't taking any chances. I just stared at him, and he quickly changed the subject. "Sorry, I'll let you know what I find about Kay."

"Thanks." It was true, it had been a while since we had a big case, and I wasn't eager for another. The last major case had put my entire family in danger, with one of them ending up in witness protection. The idea of more danger, and bullets flying toward my house, especially with Zoey home from college—*no thank you*. I preferred a safe existence. But admittedly, interesting cases did keep the job engaging, far more than paperwork, organizing my office, or staff meetings.

A FEW HOURS LATER, I flipped off the office lights and headed down the hallway. Vincent ran up to me. "Hey, Martina, heading out?"

"Yes, what did you find?"

"It's as we suspected. Kay Griffin doesn't exist. The birth certificate she gave us isn't registered in Portland, Oregon, rather Multnomah County. But her social security number is legit and everything else she told us checks out—her schools, college, address, and employment."

"Did you check surrounding counties?" Maybe she wasn't really born in Portland.

"Not yet. It's late, and most offices are closed by now."

It was nearing six in the evening. "So, all we know is that she wasn't born in Portland."

"Correct. But, if she was born somewhere else, where? Her father told her that was where she was born."

"He told her a lot of things that weren't true."

He squished up his face. "I was thinking. Maybe he was a state's witness, but didn't qualify for witness protection so he took matters into his own hands and created the new identities. If so, he would be known to the FBI and the US Marshals."

"It's possible."

"I can call my friends at the FBI and see if they can tell me anything about him."

The prospect of involving the FBI to verify Ansel and Kay's identities seemed like a necessary step. "Okay, let's get in touch with the FBI and see if they know this guy."

"I'll do that." Vincent said. "But think about it—if Ansel got a new identity fifteen years ago, wouldn't Kay remember changing her name? She was ten years old at the time. You'd think she'd have some faint recollection of a different name, right?"

"It's hard to say," I said. "Trauma can alter memories in unpredictable ways. She might not recall due to the traumatic nature of the situation, if there was one. Or more likely, her first name was always Kay and only her last name changed."

Vincent said, "True. I'll put in a call to our pals at the FBI and see what we can find out. They may or may not disclose information to us, but given that one of them is deceased, that might be enough reason for them to tell us about him."

"Great. It's getting late though. Are you sure you want to handle this tonight?"

"Yeah, Amanda's at a ceramics class, so I've got some time. Tomorrow I'll check other counties for birth records."

My gut was telling me he wouldn't find any. Considering we couldn't find Ansel Griffin tied to any marriage or birth records, we wouldn't find Kay's either. "Okay. Have a good night, and thanks, Vincent."

"Good night, boss."

As I contemplated the complexities of the case, the question loomed large: What would we find out about Ansel and Kay Griffin? And what about Kay's sister and her mother?

9

MARTINA

As I ENTERED MY HOUSE, I bent down to give Barney his obligatory scratches. These days, I couldn't go two feet without acknowledging his presence after having returned home. It had just been Barney and me since Zoey went off to college, and we'd grown closer—codependent, if you will. I never knew a dog would become such an important part of my life. When I wasn't hanging with the little furball, I would visit with Hirsch and Kim or Mom and Ted. And, of course, there was Charlie. It wasn't a huge social circle, but it was solid. And they helped me miss Zoey a little less when she was away at school.

Just thinking about Charlie got my head swimming with what could happen in just a few weeks. Not that one year with no dating was a hard and fast rule within the program, but it was a recommended amount of time, and I didn't want to compromise Charlie's road to recovery. He was such a good person, lost in drugs for so many years, with demons that continued to haunt him, namely his daughter, whom he barely spoke to. I encouraged him to seek her out, to talk to her, to let her know that he was back in the program. But Charlie was stubborn. After disappointing her in the past, he insisted he wanted to wait to prove to her that he was ready, and his sobriety would stick this time. He said once he had that one-year chip, he would reach out and hopefully, she'd be happy to hear from him.

Zoey sauntered down the hall as I shut the door behind me.

"Hey, Mom."

"Hi, Zoey. How was your day?"

"Good. Just pretty much hung out with Barney and watched TV. Do you have plans tonight with your *friend*?" She raised her hands and did air quotes. "Or are you staying in tonight?"

"Well, I was going to see if maybe you wanted to watch a movie, or we could order pizza, kind of like we used to do."

Zoey smiled. "Sure. I mean, there's a party over at Kaylie's, but not until like 10."

"Well, that's past my bedtime."

"I figured, so yeah, let's order pizza. Hey, we can even go to the store and get ice cream. Are you eating ice cream these days?"

"Not every day, but I do enjoy it from time to time."

"Good, 'cause I'm jonesing for some mint chocolate chip. Oh, and a mushroom and olive pizza and, of course, your chicken salad, right, Mom?"

"Sounds good." My precocious teenage daughter seemed to think she had it all figured out, especially when it came to knowing my favorite pizza order. Gone were the days of our Friday night movie nights, when we picked a movie, cuddled on the couch with Barney, ate pizza, and she drank soda. I didn't touch the stuff personally, but we had our ice cream for dessert. It was a tradition for so long that it became ingrained in our routine. As Zoey became a teenager and started having more plans with friends that took precedence over hanging out with her old mom. I understood it was normal and healthy, but it stung a little.

I didn't complain to her, but I did miss having Zoey around and the days when she thought I was the greatest thing in the world and always wanted to be by my side. Now, she was independent, and it seemed like she didn't need me at all.

"You know, you could invite your friend over to join us," Zoey added.

"That's okay. We have lunch plans tomorrow." As much as I'd love to see Charlie, I also wanted to spend time with my daughter and share moments with her like we used to. Sitting on the couch with Barney snuggled between the two of us, I asked, "So, big party at Kaylie's?"

"Just a few of us home from school. The old crew, you know, Kaylie, Todd, Jackson, Morgan, and Alex."

"The old high school crew," I said. "Sounds like fun."

"Yeah, it should be. Kaylie's been texting me all day about it. She's got a crush on Alex, apparently."

"Really?"

"I know, I told her it's like you've known him your whole life, and now, all of a sudden, you think he's a dreamboat."

"A dreamboat?" I asked, surprised by her terminology.

"Yeah, I heard Kaylie's mom say it once; it means like a super hot guy. But from like a hundred years ago."

"That's what I've heard too." Curious, I said, "How about you? Any guys you met at school, or girls, or a romantic interest?"

"No, not yet. There have been a few interesting guys, but I don't know, they're really not like *the one*, you know? I'm not really interested in these casual hook-ups like a lot of my friends are doing." She paused and looked at me as if she had said something she shouldn't have.

I smiled. "It's okay, I understand what college kids do."

"Oh, okay. Well, I'm not really into that, you know. And every party we go to, it's like everybody gets drunk, and then..." She paused again, looking at me, stricken.

"I also understand that college kids drink, Zoey." Did my daughter, all of a sudden, with a year of college under her belt, think her mother knew nothing of the world?

"Well, anyway, people get buzzed and hook up just randomly. Like, I had a friend go to a party, and she just made out with this guy right on the porch. She didn't even know his name, and we went home, and she never talked to him again. Gross, right?"

"It's not something I would do, but it's somewhat normal."

"Well, it's not for me. If I date someone, I want him to be my boyfriend, you know, like you and—"

"We're just friends, Zoey."

"Come on, Mom, everybody knows he's not just your friend. Maybe you guys haven't started a relationship officially, but come on, does he have any other friends like you in his life?"

Zoey had me there. "No, and we're good friends, but we're waiting before crossing any lines." I tried to explain, though I could see she wasn't entirely convinced.

"But you're pretty much together, you're just not touching each other." She wrinkled up her face, as if the mere thought of her mother touching another human being was something awful.

"We'll see what happens."

Changing the subject, Zoey said, "So, you're home relatively early. You must not be working on a very difficult case."

The case was strange but not necessarily easy. "Actually, it's quite peculiar. Vincent is the lead, trying to learn the details of this man's life, including his real identity. Vincent is reaching out to his contacts at the FBI, on the hush-hush to see if they know him," I said. "So, at this point, it's mostly background checks and a paper exercise."

"His real identity? What does that mean?"

I sat back and explained the case to her, about how a young woman came to us wanting to find her sister and her mother's graves because her father had passed away and didn't leave any documentation behind. Only to learn later that he wasn't who he said he was.

Her eyes widened. "Wow, that's crazy. I can't imagine just one day learning you aren't who you think you are. This whole time she thought she was Kay Griffin?"

"Yeah, it's on her birth certificate, which we don't believe is real."

"How awful. Does she have friends and family to support her during this time?"

My Zoey always cared so much about others, showing such empathy and love for her fellow humans and animals alike. "She has some good friends. I offered her names of different counseling services that we recommend to help her through. This is quite the revelation."

"I'd say."

My phone vibrated on the coffee table. "Is that Charlie?" Zoey asked in a teasing voice.

I picked it up and glanced at the screen. "It's work. Let me grab this, okay?"

"Okay." Zoey turned her attention to Barney, who was enjoying lying on his back getting his belly scratched. He'd been such a happy pup since Zoey came home from school.

"This is Martina."

"Martina, it's Dr. Scribner. We finished the autopsy on Ansel Griffin."

"Oh?"

"You were right. He's not Ansel Griffin."

"Were you able to match his fingerprints to somebody on file?"

"We sure did."

Finally, we were about to learn the true identity of Ansel Griffin and uncover what he'd been hiding all these years.

10

KAY

BECKY WAS HUNCHED over her laptop, determined to become my own personal private investigator, to learn more about the reasons my father could've had for changing his identity and never telling me about it. Was he hiding from someone dangerous? Or was he someone dangerous?

Reflecting back on my childhood, I wasn't sure. He never hit me; there was no physical abuse. Not really. I guess that was debatable. The punishments, which I thought were creative, were harsh. Whenever I disobeyed him, I had to go into the closet, which I always hated. It was dark and scary. I never told anybody about that. There was so much about my childhood I had blocked away and tried not to think about—like looking into his eyes when I knew I had done something wrong. He'd had the ability to instill boot-shaking fear with just a look.

Becky said, "So, the top reasons why somebody would change their identity are as follows. First, protection from threats. It says here individuals facing threats, such as domestic violence, stalking, harassment...may change their identity to escape their aggressors and start anew in safety. Second, witness protection. In the context of legal and criminal matters, witnesses to crimes, especially those involved in organized crime or facing serious threats, may be offered a new identity to protect them from potential retaliation. Third, debt escape. So, if they owe a lot of money, they might go on the run. Fourth, starting over. Usually, people who have a troubled history or simply want to leave an old life behind. Fifth, privacy. Sixth, transitioning gender, but I don't think that applies to your dad, so we can probably rule that out. Seventh, cultural or religious reasons. Eighth, professional reasons." She sat back and cocked her head. "Oh my gosh, what if your dad was an informant for the mob? He witnessed something dangerous and so he had to change his whole life. Maybe he lied to protect you."

"It's possible."

"Is there anything from your childhood that could suggest a mob affiliation? It seems kind of like a stretch, though. I mean, he's not Italian, but you probably don't have to be Italian to get on the wrong side of the mob. I think. Truthfully, I don't know much about the mob other than what I've seen in the movies."

It didn't fit but what did I know? At that point, not much. He could have lied to me for any reason at all.

Flashbacks to me and Sissy under the covers, with Sissy saying she had to hide from the monsters, never explaining more about these "monsters." I never questioned it. But who were the monsters Sissy talked about and was clearly afraid of?

Who was my dad? Who was he hiding from? All the things from my childhood I buried—the abruptness of Sissy's departure, Dad telling me I couldn't cry, that she was gone and there was nothing we could do about it. Being punished for trying to go in the attic, sneaking cookies, or being too loud.

The closet and the fact I'd been homeschooled by him.

The investigator's questions had me thinking about all the details of my childhood and how odd they were. If somebody else was telling me their story and it matched mine, I would think something was very wrong. Like not having friends as a child, not going out and meeting other kids my age.

Dad was all I had.

When he'd go to work, I was all by myself. I never had babysitters. He would put out crackers, bananas, and sandwiches—peanut butter and jelly, my favorite. He laid out all my food every day before he left, so I wouldn't be hungry. That was nice, right? Or super weird?

"Where did you go?" Becky asked, waving her arms in the air.

Feeling sick to my stomach, I said, "Just thinking back, having these flashbacks and scenes from my childhood. I don't think I'd be surprised if I learned my dad wasn't such a good guy."

"I hate to speak ill of the dead, but I got a weird vibe from your dad. I know he's your dad, and I'm sorry, but I did."

"You know, there's so much I buried in my mind. It's all flooding back. And it's all strange. Did you know that I didn't have a single friend before I was ten years old?"

Becky nodded with a look of pity. "You have plenty of friends now, and whatever the private investigators find, we'll get through it together. You have me, you have our other friends. We've all got your back."

"Thanks."

"Okay, let's do some more searching here. Supposedly, he's from Portland, Oregon. Let's see what we can find," she said with gusto, ready to dive back into the mystery of my life. "I'll Google your dad."

The private investigators couldn't find anything, so I doubted Becky could, but it felt good to think we were doing something to learn the truth. I was grateful she was taking the driver's seat because, honestly, I was too scared of what I might find.

11

MARTINA

AFTER THE REVELATION from Dr. Scribner the evening before, Vincent and I decided to deliver the news to Kay in person. We found ourselves seated in her apartment early on a Saturday morning, both of us on the sofa while Kay occupied a fluffy armchair across from us.

"It's bad, isn't it?" Kay's voice was tinged with apprehension. "You wouldn't come here on a Saturday morning if it was good news, right?"

"It's not necessarily good or bad, but it is news," I tried to reassure her.

Her roommate, Becky, walked into the living room and placed a cup of tea in front of me and water for Vincent. "I just made some homemade fudge. Would you like a piece?" she offered warmly.

After all the ice cream Zoey and I had indulged in the day before, I was off sweets for the morning. "No thank you, Becky. That's very kind of you."

"How about you, Vincent? It's pretty good if I do say so myself," Becky persisted with a smile.

Vincent smiled back. "Twist my arm."

She handed him a napkin, allowing him to choose one from the plate she was holding. As Vincent took a bite, he moaned, signaling it was quite tasty. I found myself reconsidering my stance on no fudge in the morning. Becky eyed me questioningly. "Are you sure?"

I shrugged, giving in. "Okay, I'll have one."

After serving me my piece of fudge, Becky went over to Kay, who shook her head. "No, I'm too nervous."

"It'll calm your nerves, trust me," Becky encouraged, and Kay took a piece of fudge.

As we sat there eating chocolate fudge, we were delaying the inevitable. After savoring the delightful morsel, I said, "You could open your own shop. It's delicious."

"Thank you. Maybe one day I will. Who knows, perhaps as a second career," Becky said before she set the plate down and took the armchair next to Kay.

After wiping her lips with a paper napkin, Kay said, "Okay, I'm ready."

I began. "I spoke with the medical examiner last night. She's a friend and somebody Vincent and I have both worked with at the CoCo County Sheriff's Department. We've both been consultants off and on over the years; that's how I was able to make the connection with her." I slowed down, noticing Kay was listening intently. "The autopsy revealed that your father did die from a heart attack. There doesn't appear to be any sign of foul play. Now that the autopsy is complete, the coroner's office will be calling you when they're ready to release his body for the memorial."

Kay nodded. "So, he basically died of natural causes."

"It appears so," I confirmed.

"And did they find out who he really is?" she asked.

"They did. Dr. Scribner and her team took fingerprints and some tissue samples, which helped confirm that there was nothing amiss with his autopsy or in his blood work. But the fingerprints did reveal a match to a Dr. Sidney Thomas."

"My dad's name is really Sidney Thomas? And he had been a doctor? Does that mean I'm really Kay Thomas?" Kay asked, grappling with the information.

When I'd called Vincent with the news, he had stayed late at the office again and conducted a thorough background check on Sidney "Sid" Thomas. According to the records, Sidney had been married and practiced medicine for four years before leaving town. "Yes, he was a psychiatrist. But unfortunately, we weren't able to find any records for a Kay Thomas."

"Okay, what about my mom and my sister? Did you learn anything about them?" Kay asked, clearly eager for more information.

"We did find a marriage certificate for Sidney Thomas and a Sinead Thomas. Her maiden name was Johnson," I explained.

Kay leaned in and asked, "Was she my mother?"

"We haven't been able to dig that deep yet. We'll need to confirm if she's related to you. From the photos you brought us, Sinead may be your father's first wife. The blonde woman with blue eyes. Or she could be the second wife, presumably your and your sister's mother." Saying it aloud made me realize it was odd we'd only found one marriage certificate. But there was still a lot of information and databases we'd need to search before we knew everything about Sidney Thomas.

Kay nodded slowly. "So, Sinead may not be my mother."

Shaking my head, I said, "Are you sure your mother and father were married?"

She shrugged. "I'm not sure of anything anymore."

That was a no. "Did your father say they had been married?"

"He did." She looked away. "I'm guessing you didn't find any records for my sister."

"Not yet. We still have a lot of work to do."

"Was he from Portland, Oregon, at least?"

"The records we found were from Redmond, Washington. And based on the public records, it appears that your father had lived in Washington the majority of his life. During that time, he was a practicing psychiatrist but stopped working in that field after four years, when he appears to have left Washington state," I explained.

Kay's eyes welled with tears. "He said I was born in Portland. Was anything he told me true?"

Thankfully, she wasn't alone; Becky had her arm around Kay, offering comfort.

"I know this is a lot to take in, and we're certainly not done looking into the case. We will get you answers, but it will take some time."

"Did you look for Sinead's grave? In case she was my mother?" Kay asked with hope.

"Not yet. We still have a lot of work to do to put all the pieces together. But we didn't want to delay the update about your father," I explained, trying to balance transparency with sensitivity.

We had checked the records but couldn't find a death certificate for Sinead Johnson or Sinead Thomas, especially considering Kay's father had said her mother died during childbirth. It was likely that Sinead wasn't Kay's mother. Or her father had lied about her death. Or their marriage.

"So, what's next?" Kay asked with tears in her eyes.

Vincent said, "We have requested the marriage certificate, which typically lists the parents of the bride and groom. From there, we'll try to contact them and see what they can tell us."

"He said they were dead..." Kay's voice trailed off. She shook her head in disbelief. "But then again, he told me he was a psychiatrist and named Ansel Griffin."

A partial truth. He had been a psychiatrist but was no longer. The best liars peppered in truth to make their stories more believable. "Knowing his true identity will help us find answers. But I have to warn you, it's going to take time. We'll keep you updated every step of the way. But please be patient with us."

The truth was, we could potentially have the case closed by Monday if we were able to locate birth records for Kay and her sister as well as death certificates for the two. However, if we couldn't, we were looking at a whole different ball game. The lies and secrecy that Ansel, or rather Sidney, had woven into his life made me suspect that resolving this case wouldn't be straightforward. Vincent's intuition was probably right; we might need more help to get answers as quickly as possible.

Kay nodded. "Yes. Thank you so much. This is all so overwhelming." Her words broke off as tears spilled down her cheeks. Becky quickly fetched a box of tissues and handed them to Kay.

Once calm, Kay said, "I can be patient. I had no idea who Dad really was. Looking back now, his refusal to ever speak a word about his past strikes me as not normal. And now, memories are flooding back that feel so strange."

Becky, ever the supportive friend, gently asked, "Do you want me to tell them?"

Kay nodded.

Curious, I said, "Tell us what?"

Becky's expression turned serious. "Kay's been having memories from her childhood. She mentioned she never had a friend until she was ten years old because her dad would only ever let her play in the back yard. She never went out to restaurants or left the house until they moved to Pleasant Hill. Sissy was her only friend that she can remember. And when Kay was in trouble, he would lock her in the closet."

I couldn't hide my shock. "I'm so sorry," I gasped.

Kay whispered, her voice barely audible, "He was very strict."

"Is there anything else you can tell us that you remember?"

"Sissy used to tell me we had to hide from the monsters," Kay revealed. "She never explained the monsters, just that we had to hide from them. Now, with everything coming to light, I have to wonder what really happened to her. She was fine one day and gone the next—at least, that's what my memories from when I was six tell me."

Hearing this, my stomach churned. Locked in a closet. No connection to the outside world. A child abruptly gone. My gut was telling me we had only scratched the surface of the story of Ansel Griffin, who he was, and whom he'd been hiding from.

12

MARTINA

Glancing up from my phone, I waved Vincent inside my office. "Who are you messaging with?" he asked curiously.

"Why?" I countered, a bit defensively.

"Because you have a smile on your face."

Oh. Not a surprise, I had been texting Charlie. We had shared such a great lunch and a walk around the park on Saturday. And he had agreed to let me take him out to dinner after he received his one-year chip. It would be our first official date. Zoey, and everyone else around me, knew I was in love with him. But we had never shared our feelings for each other, not wanting to cross that line, even though there was no way to step back at this point. "I was just texting my friend Charlie," I admitted to Vincent, trying to keep my tone casual.

Vincent winked. "Oh, right. Your 'friend' Charlie. How is he doing?"

"He's doing pretty good. Next week, he gets his one-year chip," I replied, feeling a mix of pride and happiness for him.

Vincent smiled widely. "Are the two of you planning to do anything to celebrate?"

"As a matter of fact, yes," I said, feeling those butterflies Charlie set off on a regular basis.

"I'm happy for him and for you too, Martina."

I still felt that silly grin on my face that Vincent had pointed out. "Anyhow, what's up?" I asked, trying to shift the conversation to work matters.

"Well, we still haven't gotten the marriage certificate, but it should be coming in the next 48 hours. I asked them to expedite it. But I did learn some things about our friend Sidney Thomas, a.k.a. Ansel Griffin."

"What did you find?"

"Well, I had a conversation with our friends at the FBI. There's no record of him being a state's witness, which means he's hiding from something or someone, but we have no idea who or why."

I had a feeling, from the sounds of Kay's childhood, that he could be an abusive person, controlling, maybe even narcissistic. It wasn't sitting right with me.

"Anything else?"

"Yes, would you like another dead end?" Vincent said, half-jokingly.

It was going to be one of those Mondays. The weekend had been so calm and quiet. Lunch and a walk with Charlie, dinner over at my mom's, visiting with her and Ted and Zoey too. Zoey had given up her Saturday night to hang out with us "old folks." On Sunday, Zoey and I took Barney to the park like we used to do. "My favorite," I said sarcastically.

"I thought you'd think so. It's not a Monday without a dead end," Vincent joked.

Wasn't that the truth. "So, what is it?" I pressed.

"Well, I dug deeper into Sinead Johnson—Sinead Thomas, married to Dr. Sidney Thomas thirty-two years ago. I was doing a record search on her and him, continuing down unconventional avenues. I looked up divorce records, considering Kay had brought in two photo albums with pictures from two different marriages. I had a hunch."

"And?" I urged, eager to hear more.

"I found a divorce decree for Sinead Johnson and Sidney Thomas, a year after their marriage."

"Short-lived, huh?" I remarked, processing the new information.

"Yeah. I thought maybe she'd have some stories to tell us. I did a search—no trace of her after she divorced Sidney."

"Nothing? Her social security number hasn't been used?"

"Nope."

"Is it possible she died?"

"It's possible, and at this point, most likely."

That was an odd statement. Everything about this case was peculiar, and "peculiar" didn't usually lead to unexpectedly happy outcomes. Usually, it was quite the opposite. "Why do you say that?"

"Because she was reported missing shortly after her divorce was finalized. I found her in the NamUs database."

I wasn't sure I would have thought to check the National Missing and Unidentified Persons System. Thankfully, Vincent had. An unsettling thought crossing my mind. Had Sidney killed his ex-wife? "Did they suspect Sidney in the missing person's case?"

"I'm glad you asked." Vincent set a file down on my desk. "According to the missing person's report, the police did question him, but he had an airtight alibi. Says he was working at the hospital the day she went missing. But this was thirty-one years ago. They didn't have cameras like they do now. He could have lied."

"How did the investigators corroborate his alibi?"

"The notes in the file say they asked his secretary."

Not exactly airtight. "Is the secretary's information listed in the report?"

"It is."

That was one person I certainly would like to talk to, assuming she was still alive.

"Anything else interesting in the report?" I flipped open the folder and started reading. It was from Redmond, Washington. According to the missing person's report, Sinead Johnson, or Sinead Thomas, had been a nurse with no children, only married the one time. Sinead didn't have any living parents. It was a coworker who reported her missing when she hadn't shown up for work for several days. I looked up at Vincent. "Did you go through the whole thing?"

"I did. Sounds like she had no living relatives when she married him and then died, or went missing, I should say, shortly after she left him."

"Anything in the divorce papers?"

"Nothing. Just cited irreconcilable differences."

"Any reports of abuse?"

"No, but the report does say that her coworker, the one who reported her missing, saw bruises. Sinead always told her it was an accident at home, that she was clumsy, but the friend suspected there was something off about Sidney."

I was beginning to agree with his ex-wife's former coworker's assessment.

All these pieces of Sidney's life weren't adding up to a very pretty picture, and I wondered what that meant for Kay. "We need to learn everything about Sidney Thomas and find the information for his second wife, presumably Kay's mother…" I stopped my thought and said, "But if his first wife went missing and never had children, the second wife would have to be the sister's mother, the one in the second photo album. Or even a third if Sissy and Kay had different mothers.

Honestly, we can't trust any of the information Ansel told Kay."

"Exactly. And why isn't there another marriage record for the second wife? There is clearly a second wedding album."

An excellent point. "It's possible he was using another name before he became Ansel Griffin."

"To hide the affiliation with the missing ex-wife?"

Maybe. "But would he give up a career after only four years, and every other part of his life, when he'd been cleared of the crime?"

Vincent cocked his head. "Cleared, but the case was never closed. Maybe a new set of investigators would have taken a closer look at him, and he'd become their main suspect, and he didn't want to risk it."

If Sidney had killed his first wife, what else had he done? "Okay, we need to dig deep on this. Especially if it could solve an old missing person's case." I may no longer be on the Cold Case Squad for CoCo County, but that didn't mean I wouldn't try to seek justice when it needed to be sought.

Vincent crossed his arms and said, "And that, boss, is why I think we need more people on this."

"I agree."

As much as we were determined to learn the truth, part of me still worried about what we'd find.

13

MARTINA

Glancing at my watch, I saw there was only an hour before I was supposed to have lunch with Hirsch. It was our weekly lunch date to catch up on life and investigations. I'd send him a quick text to reschedule for a little later. "Let's find a conference room and start mapping this out. I've got a feeling that this is a crazy spiderweb, and it might be difficult to sort out."

"My thoughts exactly. I've already reserved Conference Room Two," he said with a smile.

"All right, let's go."

Was I jumping to conclusions about the case by assuming Ansel had been involved in his first wife's disappearance? Maybe, but statistically, it was most likely. And if this man had killed his ex-wife, we would need to prove it. Her loved ones deserved to know. At the very least, we would contact the Redmond, Washington police department to ask if they had any updates on the case, if anybody was still working it, or if anybody was attempting to. We would share any and all information we uncovered. Who knows? Maybe they'd been looking for Ansel a.k.a. Sidney Thomas all along.

Inside, Vincent shut the door, picked up a dry-erase marker, and said, "Come on, let's get started."

It was times like these I missed the Cold Case Squad. A group of people with like minds but different perspectives, each coming up with a new way to look at the case. Our solve rate was unlike any other. But we had the best and brightest at Drakos Monroe too.

Vincent said, "All right, we start with what we know. First of all, we know that Sidney Thomas was born sixty-five years ago. He became a medical doctor, specializing in psychiatry, at the age of thirty. Three years later, he marries Sinead Johnson. One year later, they divorce, and Sinead goes missing. At this time, he moves out of Redmond, Washington, and quits his job at the hospital. Nobody knows his whereabouts from that point forward, until his daughter walks into our offices, and we learn he became Ansel Griffin fifteen years ago. He told Kay her mother died in childbirth and that Kay's sister, 'Sissy,' died when Kay was six. That would be nineteen years ago."

Listening to him, I realized there may be significant challenges ahead. We were looking for records and interviews from twenty to thirty years ago. Mostly before the digital age. Looking at the board, I said, "We have a gap from when Sidney Thomas ended and Ansel Griffin started. There's sixteen years when he was aged 34-50 that we haven't found any records for. That could explain why we can't find any marriage certificates, divorce, or birth records relating to Kay, her mother, and her sister. Both of the girls would've been born during the gap."

Vincent capped the marker, spun around, and said, "Exactly. So, we need to figure out where he was and what his name was during those sixteen years."

And who he married and fathered.

"We know that fifteen years ago, he started working for a medical practice as a file clerk. He stayed in the same industry as when he was a psychiatrist, so maybe during the gap years, he was also working in a hospital or a medical practice—obviously not as a psychiatrist because you have to have a lot of records and documentation for that."

"So, we check every hospital in the United States during those sixteen years?" Vincent said, before shaking his head. "No. We can start with facial recognition. We know he had a driver's license in California. We just have to check other states," Vincent said, his eyes wide with excitement.

Brilliant.

A small smile formed on my lips. "And that's why we like you, Vincent."

"It's not my charming personality? It's *just* my keen investigation skills?"

"Can it be both?"

"I'll allow it."

I said, "Good. We can start in Oregon. If Sidney's other half-truths mean anything, maybe when he told Kay she was born in Oregon, it was the truth. Maybe that was where he went after Washington." It wasn't a big leap to assume he may have gone from living in Washington to Oregon and then eventually settled into California, just heading south each time he needed to flee and create a new identity.

Vincent said, "Smart. I'll start checking DMV photos for the state of Oregon. Hopefully it doesn't take too long and they have the digital records."

"We might just figure this out after all." Not that I'd doubted it, but I worried how long it might take.

"I think so, but it may not be so straightforward."

"What are you thinking?" I asked.

"If he was living in Oregon for those sixteen years, we may need to go up there, talk to anybody who knew him, and the same for here in the Bay Area. But I've got a hunch his last identity before he came to California will give us the most answers."

I was inclined to agree with him.

That sixteen-year gap could be the key to who Sidney Thomas had become, who he was hiding from, and why. Was it simply because he was a person of interest in a missing person's case, which, based on the file I'd read, didn't look like he was much of a suspect anymore. But maybe it was enough to spook him. He went on the run, changed identities, got married, and had children...it could fit a man worried he'd be implicated in a murder.

But something else was nagging at me.

How had he acquired his new identity? He had been, from all accounts, an upstanding citizen, a doctor. How would someone like that, who was living on the right side of the law, create such an elaborate new identity that nobody had been able to crack until now?

"And you didn't find a criminal history for him, right?"

Vincent shook his head. "No, clean as a whistle until he, well, disappeared and changed his identity. But even as Ansel Griffin, clean as a whistle."

How had he known how to change his identity with such realistic documentation? "We should talk to Kay, find out about the memorial service. If she runs the announcement in the newspaper, maybe somebody will show up who can provide some insight into his past."

"Do you think people may come out of the woodwork to pay their respects?" Vincent pondered.

"It's possible."

"All right, boss. I guess I've got myself a busy Monday."

"Can you handle it all? We can pull in a few others. And I'm ready to get my hands dirty." I stopped and thought about it. "Or how about this? I'll pick up the background on Ansel Griffin, you'll investigate the sixteen-year gap since that's the trickiest, and I'll find another member of the team to keep digging into Sidney Thomas. The three of us will work together to have the full picture of who this guy was and who he had in his life. This should lead to answering Kay's original questions regarding her mother and sister's graves. And maybe we'll also learn what happened to Sinead."

"Solid plan. That's why you're the boss. If I need help, I'll let you know. Otherwise, let's meet tomorrow. Oh nine hundred."

Should I be worried that Vincent was quoting military time? Had his time at Drakos Monroe turned him into ex-military by proxy?

"Oh nine hundred. I'll call Kay. And get someone to take over the Sidney Thomas history. I want to know everything we can about this guy." My gut was screaming at me that there was a lot to learn.

"Sounds good. I'll get into the nitty-gritty and find out his identity during the gap years and who he married and fathered. By the end of this, we're going to know more about this guy than he did."

Yes, we will.

14

KAY

Shaking my head, I couldn't believe the news. How could I not have known? My dad, the only family I had ever known, was named Sidney Thomas. Then, when he met my mother and I was born, for sixteen whole years, he had a different identity. How could I not have known? It was so strange. I was glad I had hired the private investigator, but when I did, I had no idea I would learn my father wasn't who he said he was. Confident the investigators would find my mom and my sister's graves, I was grateful, but I also felt a little lost and like I had no idea who I was anymore.

"What did they say?" Becky asked.

"They think he had more than two identities and that when I was born, he had a different name and changed it again fifteen years ago."

I could tell Becky was trying her best not to look shocked or horrified, but I knew that was how she felt. We'd lived together for two years, having been friends for far more.

"Sorry to hear that, Kay. Maybe if we continue going through your dad's old stuff, or try to get into his computer, we'll be able to learn more." She hesitated, looked at me, and asked, "Are you all right?"

Was I? I stood in my father's living room, looking across at the sofa and the television, his desk in the corner, the entry to the kitchen, the bathroom down the hall, my childhood bedroom on the right, the spare room on the left. Dad's room was upstairs. Did he even own the house? Was it possible he didn't?

Could you buy a house with a fake ID? The PIs said it was a sophisticated identity, and that was how he was able to live undetected with somebody else's name, somebody else's social security number.

There was a pit forming in my stomach. My thoughts turned back to Sissy. I had pushed away the memories for so long, but now she was all I could think about.

Had she really died?

What about my mother?

Was she dead?

Maybe what my dad said was true. He was so sad about the past he had to start completely fresh. I remembered moving after Sissy died, very shortly after, actually.

Memories I had repressed came back: waking the next morning, asking Daddy what happened to her, where she was. His face had been red. He was angry, or sad, or... He wasn't his calm, cool self. Something had happened, and I had, at the time, questioned for a second if she had died. He was grief-stricken, worried, shaky. Even at six years old, I could understand that what had happened was serious.

I begged Dad to let me keep all her things, but he wouldn't let me. Instead he boxed them up and took them away as if she never existed. Why had he done that?

I wasn't much younger than she was. I could've worn her

clothes, played with her toys, or read her books. Why would he take them away from me?

What else had he lied about?

Did I have living relatives? What about his friends? Who were they?

Over the years, he had people—men—come over. They usually didn't come over more than once and were sort of the same nondescript, middle-aged white man. They just reminded me of my dad. I never thought much of it, but Dad had never dated or tried to find someone new. Why not?

Before I could turn my attention back to Becky, a knock sounded on the door. Becky said, "Are you expecting someone?"

I shook my head. "No, as far as I know, nobody ever comes by." Did I really know that? I hadn't lived at home since I was eighteen. As soon as I went to college, I had moved into the dorm and then after the first year moved to off-campus housing with friends. The school and my apartment were only a twenty-minute drive from Dad's, so there was no reason for me to move home during the summers. He didn't seem to mind.

I scurried toward the door and looked through the peephole. It was a man, middle-aged, with dark hair and glasses.

"Who is it?" Becky asked.

"I don't know, it's just some man."

Becky held up her cell phone. "Okay, I'm ready to dial 911 if it's a threat." She had been watching too many episodes of Dateline and serial killer documentaries.

I opened the door, and the man flinched to see me, like he wasn't expecting me. That was good—it meant he likely wasn't there to hurt me. Yet, all of a sudden, I was afraid for my safety. I was never paranoid before, but all this news about my dad had me on edge.

"Can I help you?" I asked.

"I am looking for Ansel. Does he live here?"

Becky stepped forward, likely noticing my shock and inability to say the words. "Ansel passed away a week ago. Can we help you with something?"

"Oh, no, I'm sorry to hear that. Were you close?" He looked us up and down, and I didn't like the feeling. It felt like he was checking us out, and he was far too old for that. Goosebumps went down my spine.

"I'm his daughter."

He stepped back and said, "I'm very sorry for your loss." And he turned to walk away.

I couldn't help but go after him. "Wait," I called out.

He turned his head. "Yeah?"

"How did you know my dad?"

He quickly said, "We worked together."

"At the medical center?"

The man looked confused. "Oh, yeah." He nodded.

He was lying to me. He didn't work at the medical practice. Who was this man, and now that I really thought about it, who were the other men? If my memories were right, they were always different. Never the same one twice.

"What's your name?" I pressed.

"My name is Joe. Like I said, I'm sorry for your loss." He hurried down the steps into his car and drove off before I could run after him.

It was someone who knew my dad. Maybe he knew why Dad changed his name. I didn't believe he worked at the medical center, but I wasn't sure. I would have to go down there and ask if there was someone named Joe working with my dad who matched the description of this man. That could help me find the truth.

Standing on my front porch, I thought back to the other men. If they were not colleagues, like "Joe," then who were they? Was Dad part of some secret society I knew nothing about?

"That was strange," Becky said.

"We need to go to my dad's work. See if that guy really works there."

"Yeah, let's do it. First thing tomorrow morning."

"Okay."

We went back inside, locking the door behind us, and walked back into the living room. Becky sat down and said, "And what are you thinking about for the memorial? Should we call the funeral home now that the body's been released?"

I shook my head. "No, I don't even know who he was. How can I have a memorial for someone when I don't know? With all these other identities, I have to know the truth first. I can't lay him to rest if I can't even say who he was."

"But what about the body?"

"I've decided. I'll have him cremated. That way, we have more time for the memorial, and it seems like a reasonable option."

Becky nodded. "Good idea. With that settled, we should keep going through all his things. Maybe he didn't keep all of his important papers in the attic. We need to look everywhere for clues and records of his life. Including the deed to the house and his car information. See if he has a will. If we can break into his computer, maybe we can learn more about who he was."

"Smart. So, what did you find online about hacking into computers?"

She lifted the lid to her laptop and said, "I'll show you."

Martina and Vincent seemed to be good at their jobs, but there were some things that we could do. It made me feel more in control to do something on my own.

15

MARTINA

After a warm embrace, I looked into Hirsch's sparkling blue eyes and said, "Thanks for meeting me."

He nodded, a hint of intrigue in his gaze. "I figured you must have an interesting case if it's keeping you at the office this late."

"Oh, it's interesting, all right." I explained the complexities of the investigation into Sidney Thomas, a.k.a. Ansel Griffin, a.k.a. an unknown entity for sixteen years.

He shook his head in disbelief. "I swear, you're a magnet for this stuff. It doesn't matter where you are, whether at CoCo County or at your firm."

"It's a gift, I suppose. Maybe God is sending them my way, knowing that I will stop at nothing to find the truth."

"That may be it."

As the conversation deepened, I found myself considering how many of these tough cases landed in my lap. I'd solved each one. Maybe it was my purpose and why God had given me a second chance so many years ago, when I almost died after a drunk driving accident. I was put on this earth to deliver justice, to find the truth. Unfortunately, sometimes the truth hurts innocent people. And I had a feeling the more we learned about Kay's father, the more it would hurt her.

"How are things at CoCo County?" I asked, shifting the topic.

"They're having a heckuva time with Leslie's cases."

"Any work on new cases?"

He shook his head. "Nope, it's all about trying to defend Leslie's cases. Checking every 'i,' crossing every 't.' It's painful."

It had been hurtful when we were betrayed by Leslie, a once valued member of the Cold Case Squad. Now, so many criminals could go free because she'd worked the case, and everything she worked on throughout her entire career could be put into question. "I'm sorry you're having to go through that. How are Kim and Audrey?"

"Audrey's doing great. She's enrolled in half a dozen summer camps. Because, of course, she wanted to be in every art class they offered."

I smiled. No doubt, that was Zoey's influence when she used to babysit Audrey quite regularly.

"How's Zoey?"

"She's doing well. She's home and visiting with all her friends. Most of them had gone away to different schools, so she's making up for lost time. Basically, she's living her best life."

"Must be nice. Carefree college kid. Nothing but fun on the agenda."

"Yeah, well, she deserves it. She works hard at school. First year, not a single B."

"That doesn't surprise me. She was always years ahead."

With a wistful smile, I said, "I always wondered how she could be my daughter."

"You sell yourself short, Martina. You may not have a

college degree, but you are one of the smartest and most clever people I've ever met."

"Hirsch, are you trying to make me cry?"

"Yes."

I chuckled. "Thanks."

"And how's Charlie?"

I was wondering when Hirsch would mention him. "He's doing really well, excited about his one-year sobriety anniversary next week."

"I bet he's not the only one excited. What are you two planning to do to celebrate?"

"Dinner."

"Nice choice." He nodded. "I knew when you introduced him at Thanksgiving last year he was special."

"What are you talking about? We haven't been on a date yet; we're just friends," I protested as Hirsch started laughing.

"Martina, you forget who you're talking to. I've been your partner for how long now? A decade, off and on. I know you. Charlie is a great guy. I think he's good for you. Not who I would've pictured, but after meeting him and talking to him, I think he's a great match for you."

Hirsch could always see right through me, and I knew better than to argue. "I hope so. I haven't felt like this about anybody in so long that I'm almost overwhelmed by it," I confessed.

"That's how you know. Have you met his daughter yet?" he asked.

"No. She's pretty headstrong and upset that her father left her when he was still struggling with drugs and alcohol. He's come back sober before, so he's hesitant to reach out again. He wants to hit his one-year mark and then try again."

"That's rough. I can't imagine," Hirsch sympathized.

"Me too. It made me think about how my relationship with Zoey could've been if I hadn't gotten sober. Would she have hated me, refused to talk to me?" I said. "Charlie is such a good soul, but I didn't know him when he was using. And I'm not his daughter who surely had wanted a sober, present, and loving parent. Addicts have a hard time with that. Charlie said his daughter, Selena, is headstrong and independent, probably learning to be that way in order to protect herself. It's sad. I certainly hope to meet her one day."

"I'm sure you will. And children have a way of being very forgiving."

It was true. "I hope so."

"So, what are you thinking about the case?"

"The description of his behavior from the daughter during her younger years makes me think he's hiding something big. We're going to ask her if we could take a look at her father's computer, try to get inside, see what we can find. When I spoke with her earlier, she said she was looking through the house to find any kind of information she could. And that she didn't want to have the memorial until she knew who he was, his whole story."

"That's rough. I can't imagine what she's going through. Does she have support?" Hirsch asked.

"Friends."

"That's good." He hesitated, then added, "Have you come up with any theories about this guy? My brain is connecting all kinds of dots that could be leading to a picture of a bad man."

My gut was saying the same thing, but I wanted to know more before I shared some of those suspicions. "I have a few, but at this point, he could be anywhere on the spectrum from violent criminal to deep undercover."

Kay's accounts of her childhood, being locked in the closet and her seclusion from the rest of the world until she was ten, made me lean toward the criminal side of the rainbow.

"Well, you know if CoCo County somehow needs to get involved, we'll prioritize it."

"Famous last words."

"Oh, great. I've just jinxed it, haven't I? Well, I'll take a breath before the latest Martina Monroe investigation rains down on CoCo County."

With a grin, I thought to myself, *we'll see.*

—

16

LIA

My smile was wide as I was surrounded by my mom, dad, grandma, and grandpa. It was one of the happiest days of my life. Graduating from medical school was a monumental achievement. I had worked so hard for so long, yet I couldn't help but feel that my smile wasn't quite wide enough. After all those years of study and sacrifice, I thought I would feel lighter, freer. I had accomplished something huge, but it didn't fill me up like I'd anticipated. There was still something missing.

For many years, I had thrown myself into school, perhaps as a distraction from what I wasn't supposed to talk about.

Mom and Dad swore up and down that I'd never had a sister, insisting that the little girl from my childhood memories was likely an imaginary friend, as my childhood psychiatrist had suggested.

Then why did it feel so real?

Was that how children with imaginary friends felt, as if they could truly see them? Had she been a ghost? I met a woman in medical school who had mediums in her family. She claimed she didn't possess the gift, but her grandmother did. I went to see her, trying to summon the spirit of that girl I remembered from my childhood, but we didn't reach anybody. Which meant, if she wasn't a spirit—a concept I wasn't entirely sure I believed in, including the afterlife, spirits, ghosts, and hauntings—then she must have been a figment of my imagination.

Why couldn't I accept it?

Her chubby face, her soft laugh... I had no reason to believe my family would lie to me. Grandma was the most sympathetic about it. She told me that when she was little, she had an imaginary friend too and that it was completely normal. There was nothing wrong with me, she assured. The only problem was that I didn't think she was imaginary. If she had been, why would I feel like she was a part of me?

In med school, learning about different personality disorders and mental health problems, I wondered if I was schizophrenic or had a whole other host of illnesses. It's common for med students; when you know too much, you think you have everything. But I had no other signs of schizophrenia. I didn't see other people or children. It was just *her*.

Grandma walked into the living room, breaking my train of thought. "What are you doing, Lia?"

"Just looking at the pictures from my graduation," I said as I flipped through the photo album.

"Such a proud day, honey. I'm so glad Grandpa and I were there to share it with you," she said with a smile.

"I was so happy you were there too," I said, the warmth of the memory wrapping around me like a comforting blanket.

"You look worried. Are you nervous about starting your residency?"

Her keen eyes didn't miss the shadow of concern that probably flickered across my face. I shook my head, although a part of me wondered if perhaps I should be nervous. "No, no, I just... I don't know. I don't know why I'm feeling this way."

"You know you can tell me anything, right?"

"Just this feeling that I've always had, Grandma. It's like part of me is missing, and I need to find it."

"Maybe you just haven't really found that one thing you were meant to do yet. Yes, being a doctor is absolutely your calling, and you're gonna make a great pediatrician. But what about something more? Maybe through your work with children, you'll find your calling in something like Doctors Without Borders or another specialty that you discover through your profession. Maybe that's what's missing—that really detailed purpose."

I had always thought helping people would be my purpose, that becoming a physician was the answer. But maybe Grandma was right. I wasn't feeling satisfied because I hadn't found what my true purpose was yet. I had found a part of it, but perhaps the whole picture wasn't clear yet. "Thanks, Grandma, you might be right."

"You're so young; you have your whole life ahead of you. You'll find what it is that makes you whole. I know it. I can feel it."

"Thanks, Grandma."

I hoped she was right. Maybe I would find that thing that filled in the emptiness, that elusive piece I couldn't shake off.

My thoughts drifted back to that little girl—if she wasn't imaginary and she wasn't a ghost, who was she? With a few weeks off before residency started, perhaps I could spend my time trying to figure it out.

17

MARTINA

While Vincent delved deep into the 16-year gap, I directed all my focus to the Ansel Griffin identity. For the last 15 years, he had been an upstanding citizen who seemed to keep to himself considering he had no criminal history, no marriages, and no financial woes—nothing that would raise eyebrows. But one detail I couldn't ignore was the fact that his Ansel Griffin identity was far from legal.

Crafting such a sophisticated identity isn't a feat just anyone could achieve. It made me think he may have ties with law enforcement or criminals. My instincts pulled me toward the idea he had to have been embroiled in illegal activities or closely associated with those who were. But what had he been involved in? And who were the criminals in his life?

With his paper trail proving too clean, it was time to pound the pavement and start interviewing anyone and everyone who knew him personally. The memorial service would have been a perfect opportunity for that, but since his daughter had decided to postpone the memorial service until our investigation concluded, that wasn't an avenue to explore. I couldn't blame her. How do you greet a room full of mourners you don't know, including the man being honored?

Since the memorial was out of the question for interviews, my first stop was the medical office where Ansel had worked for 15 years. Inside the psychiatry office, it was modern with small sofas arranged in small clusters in shades of grays and blues. There was only a handful of people in the waiting area.

Approaching the receptionist, I was greeted by a woman with a welcoming smile. "Hello, how may I help you?"

"My name is Martina Monroe, and I'm helping out Ansel Griffin's daughter as she plans for his memorial. Could you spare a few moments to discuss him?"

The receptionist's demeanor shifted slightly, a hint of nervousness as she glanced around. "What kind of questions do you have? Are you with the police?"

Shaking my head, I presented my business card. "His daughter has requested an exploration into his family since his passing. I'm trying to learn if anyone here might have been close to him, perhaps socially, or if they frequently had lunch together. What can you tell me about Ansel Griffin?"

She lowered her voice and her eyes met mine. "To be honest, I've only worked here for a few years, but I've heard Ansel has been here forever. Everyone says he's good at his job. He's a file clerk, and everything's always done on time. He never misses work, doesn't call in sick; he's really reliable." The discreet nature of her voice was puzzling. She spoke highly of Ansel, so the hushed tones seemed odd.

"But?" I asked.

"This is just a gut feeling—and I'm not saying this is true. Maybe it's just me—but he was kind of a loner. Didn't really talk to anybody at work. And he had this stare, like he would just look at you for a really long time. I don't know how to describe it. But he gave me the creeps."

Was the receptionist the only one who thought Ansel was creepy? "I see. And you don't think he was friends with anyone here?"

"You can ask his supervisor. I'm just at the front desk, but you can ask." She hesitated and then said, "She's in right now. I'll get her," then quickly excused herself back into the office.

A moment later, a woman in a beige pants suit appeared. "I'm Lana, the office manager. Dawn says you have a few questions about a former employee?"

"Yes, I do." I introduced myself.

"Please come with me."

With a nod, I followed her to her office. We sat down across from each other. "What questions do you have about Ansel? I hear his daughter asked you to do a background check, presumably to find more family and friends."

"Yes, something like that. Was Ansel close with anybody here who I could talk to, perhaps to make sure they know about the memorial service she'll have for him?"

Lana scrunched up her face. "You know, he was a good worker, and I'm sorry for his daughter's loss, but he wasn't close with anyone. He came in, did his job, made polite conversation in the break room, and left."

"Was there anybody he seemed to talk to more than others?"

"No, nothing more than pleasantries like 'good morning' and 'how about that weather' or 'did you catch the game this weekend?' That kind of stuff."

"Were there any complaints about him over the last fifteen years?"

She shook her head. "No, and I haven't been his supervisor for that long, but there were no complaints. However, there was sort of an overall vibe that he gave off. It was almost like an intensity. It's hard to describe, but it was unnerving at times because he was so quiet. Even when he was angry, he just...

looked like he was going to bubble up, but he never did. It sounds crass, but if he had come in one day and shot up the office, I guess I'd say, 'Oh yeah, that guy.'"

The conversation had taken a dark turn. Everyone Ansel worked with thought he was a bit off. Add that to the fact that, from Kay's description of her childhood, he had been abusive toward his daughter and that he had fake identification, and it was starting to look like Ansel Griffen a.k.a. Sidney Thomas was bad news.

"Is there anything else you can tell me about him?"

"That's about it. He didn't share much personal information. Honestly, I didn't even know he had a daughter until she called to tell us of his passing."

Puzzling. "This has been helpful. Do you mind if I speak with any other employees who worked with him?"

"It's a busy day today, so it might be tricky. The only people he crossed paths with were the receptionist, the doctors, the cleaning staff, and me. The doctors are booked today, and the cleaning crew isn't in yet. We all discussed him after we learned of his death. You know how it is. Nobody knew much about him. But I can ask again if anybody else knew him better and get back to you. I'm assuming you have a card?"

I nodded, handing her my card. "Thank you for your time."

"It was nice meeting you, Miss Monroe. I hope you find what you're looking for," Lana said kindly.

Thanking her, I felt an unease about what I had learned of Ansel's demeanor and his coworkers' view of him. Why had he kept to himself? Was he simply a recluse who had kept his daughter and himself away from the world? Or was he trying to hide his true self from his coworkers, afraid they'd learn he wasn't who he claimed?

As I walked toward the exit, my eyes caught sight of Kay

and her friend Becky. Our gazes locked. *What are they doing here?*

18

MARTINA

WITH A WAVE AND A SMILE, I approached Kay and Becky. "Hi, there. What a surprise. I didn't expect to see you here." Hopefully they got the hint that I'd like to know why they were there. I would have expected Kay to tell me if she was going to be visiting her father's former employer.

Kay looked stricken. "Hi."

"Hi, Martina. We were just checking some things," Becky said evasively.

Based on what I'd learned earlier and my suspicion that Ansel may have been on the wrong side of the law, I said, "Do you mind if we speak outside for a minute?" Not that there was anything wrong with Kay visiting her father's former place of employment; it was her secretive demeanor that seemed out of place.

Once outside, I said, "I was just interviewing some of your dad's coworkers to ask if he had any friends or anyone he was close to, to get an overall feel for how people saw your father."

"Did you find any friends, or relationships, or anything?" Becky asked.

Was Becky helping Kay launch her own investigation into

her father? "No, but his office manager said she'd call me after she asked around the office, just to be sure."

"Oh, did they tell you anything interesting?" Becky asked.

After eyeing Kay, I turned my attention back to Becky. "They say he mostly kept to himself and didn't have any friends. But they did think he seemed odd and maybe stared a lot."

Kay said, quietly, "That's what Becky said."

Becky nodded. "He always gave off an icky old man vibe."

Interesting. "Did he ever say anything or do anything inappropriate with you, Becky?"

She shook her head. "He just stared a lot. It was unnerving."

Just like his coworkers had said. "I have to ask. What are you two doing here?"

The two young women exchanged glances. They obviously had a reason they weren't sure they wanted to share with me.

Kay finally said, "A man came by my dad's house yesterday looking for him. When I told him Dad died, he just ran off and didn't want to answer any more of my questions. But I ran after him and asked him how he knew Dad. He said they worked together, and then I questioned if it was at the medical practice. He hesitated and said yes. But I didn't believe him."

"So, you came here to see if that man works here?" I clarified.

She nodded.

Not wanting to alarm Kay, I wasn't quite sure how to explain to her that investigating on her own could be dangerous. And knowing a stranger showed up at Ansel's house and left hastily, I was even more sure there was something nefarious in Ansel's past.

"You know, if you have questions like this, or if more people come by the house, my firm can take care of that for you. We can investigate; we're trained for these types of situations," I said, hoping to provide some reassurance.

"Oh, okay," she responded, somewhat relieved.

"What did the man say his name was?"

"He said it was Joe, but I think he was lying."

"What did he look like?"

"He was a middle-aged white man with dark hair and glasses."

The description didn't match anyone I had seen in the office, but I hadn't seen any of the doctors or cleaning staff.

"How about this: let me go back in there and ask if anybody who works there is named Joe. It might be better if you stay out here," I suggested, hoping to ensure her safety.

"But I'd be able to recognize him. You couldn't."

Understanding the importance of her input, I agreed, and we re-entered the office.

After introductions with the receptionist, I said, "I have another quick question. Is there a man named Joe who works here? Maybe one of the doctors or the cleaning staff?"

Dawn, the receptionist, shook her head. "Are you sure he works here?"

"No. Just checking. He's got dark hair and glasses." She didn't need to know there was an unknown man showing up at a dead man's house pretending to work there.

"Nobody by that description here. And nobody named Joe."

"Okay, thank you for your time."

As we left the office, my concern for Kay's safety deepened.

Back outside, I said, "It sounds like you were right. That man wasn't who he claimed to be. What were you doing at your father's house?"

Not that she owed me an explanation, but it would be nice to know.

"Looking for things that might help us with the investigation. Maybe it would help if you came with us. Is that something your firm could assist with? Try to find hiding spots like under floorboards and behind picture frames?" Her suspicion of her father was evident.

"Of course, I can help you sift through things and see if we can uncover anything useful that might shed light on who he was and what happened to your mother and your sister," I offered, eager to help *and* keep an eye on Kay. "Let's set up a time to do that. When would work for you?"

"It's kind of short notice, but tonight would be great." She glanced around the parking lot. "I'm off today but have to return to work tomorrow."

Her behavior struck me as odd, but before I could delve deeper, my phone rang—a call from Vincent. Deciding it could wait, I asked, "What time would you like to meet?"

"Five? Is that too late? Do you work after hours like that?" she asked.

"For something like this, absolutely. Five is fine," I reassured her.

After exchanging goodbyes, I called Vincent as I made my way back to my car. "Hey, Vincent. What's up?"

"How did it go at the medical office?" he asked.

I updated him on my findings and then said, "Did you find his missing identity?"

"I sure did."

19

MARTINA

AFTER A QUICK CALL home to Zoey to let her know I was going to be working late tonight, I headed toward the conference room where Vincent and Jerilyn were waiting for me. Vincent had made a significant discovery regarding the identity of Sidney Thomas, who had become Ansel Griffin. All Vincent told me on the phone was that he did a full background check and that it was interesting.

As I walked through the offices of Drakos Monroe, I took in the familiar sights: the faces of my colleagues, the cubicles, and the artwork on the walls. Everything here felt like home. Despite my love for working on the Cold Case Squad with Hirsch and the rest of the team—where the atmosphere was warm and the people were like family—it never truly felt like home, not in the way this place did. I waved to Stavros, who returned the gesture with a smile.

Stavros and I had been through a lot together. He had worked with my husband in the army, and he was the one who had recruited us to work for his firm. Then, later, after Jared's death, he kept an eye on Zoey and me, giving me a second chance after I nearly destroyed myself with alcohol. He provided the tough love I needed to persevere, along with the support from Zoey and my sponsor, Rocco. I owed this man so much; he continued to give even after I had spent several years away working with the CoCo County Sheriff's Department. And when I was ready to return full-time, he said he would be honored to be my business partner. Stavros was more than just a colleague—he was family and had been for longer than anyone else I knew.

Hirsch and the team had become a family over the last nine years, but Stavros wasn't just family to me and Zoey; he was also a link to Jared. As I passed him, he called out, "Hey, Martina, how's the new case going? Looks like you've got a team bustling about."

"It's turning out to be more complicated than we originally suspected," I said. "The young woman who came to us is looking for her mother and sister's graves. It turns out her father has had at least three different identities, and she didn't even know it. We haven't been able to locate her mother or her sister's graves yet."

"Do you have enough resources?"

"I'm adding them as we see fit. Jerilyn just joined our team. Each one of us is taking one of the identities and running with it. We're bringing them together to see where we can find commonalities and put together one big, clear picture to ultimately find out the truth about what happened to her mother, her sister, and frankly, even her own history."

"All right, well, I won't keep you. Good luck. If anybody can solve it, it's you and the team. Take care."

With that, I continued on to where Vincent and Jerilyn sat in the conference room, deep in discussion.

Vincent's hands were animatedly waving in the air. I knocked before entering, just so I wouldn't startle him. Upon entering, I closed the door behind me and greeted them. "Hi, Jerilyn. Hi, Vincent."

"Hey, Martina," Vincent said. "I was just telling Jerilyn about some of the crazy stuff we've found."

"It's different from the cases I normally work on," Jerilyn added. "Thanks for adding me to the team. I think I can learn a lot."

"I think so too," I responded, acknowledging Jerilyn's potential. Jerilyn was relatively new to the Drakos Monroe family but had shown promise in the last two years. We decided to have her research the Sidney Thomas identity.

Vincent said, "I've got updates, obviously, but why don't we go ahead and let Jerilyn tell you what she's found. Then, we can get into the juicy stuff."

If Vincent said it was juicy, I knew to believe him.

Jerilyn, eager to share her findings, stood up. "I've updated the board here," she began, pointing to the notes on Sidney Thomas. "Unfortunately, I haven't found anything new. Vincent and I discussed it, and we think that once we get the marriage certificate, which should arrive by tomorrow at the latest, we'll be able to reach out to family members. The parents should be listed on the certificate. If we can't find them that way, there are other methods to try to find relatives, but it's a bit trickier. But if it's needed, I'll research using a new methodology."

"Great," I said, acknowledging the plan.

"The other thing we were considering," Jerilyn continued, "is if we can get a hold of Ansel's computer, maybe we can see if there's anything on it that could help us figure out what this guy was really up to."

"I'm meeting with the daughter later this evening to help search her father's house for any records that could give us a clue about who he's been and what he's been up to. I'll ask her about it."

"And ask for a sample of her and her father's DNA?" Vincent asked.

"I can do that. Why? Did you find something interesting?" I asked, a little surprised by the request that seemed to come out of nowhere.

"The suspense is killing you, Martina," he said in a mock evil voice, making Jerilyn chuckle.

Jerilyn said, "That's pretty much all I have right now. It would be good to have the computer. We can get inside if the daughter doesn't have the password. I'm pretty good with encryption software, and if I can't crack it, the team here will be able to."

We had one of the best tech teams in the world. Cracking Ansel's laptop password would likely be child's play for them. "Good to know. Alright, Vincent, tell us what you've got."

He stood up with a flourish, twirling around before delivering the news. "The missing identity we've been waiting for—the gap of who Sidney Thomas became for 16 years before Ansel Griffin is, wait for it..." He paused, relishing the moment, which was so darn entertaining I couldn't even get annoyed. "Rex Michels, of Portland, Oregon."

"A name," I muttered, intrigued.

"And he was Rex Michels for the entire 16 years we're looking into," Vincent explained. "During that time, I found employment records, housing records, a marriage record, and a record for a child who was born to him and his wife."

"A child? Only one?" I asked.

Vincent nodded.

"What did he do for work?"

"He was a file clerk at a local hospital."

It fit. "Is the hospital still around?"

"Yep, so that's one potential source of people to interview if we need to."

"Okay, what else have you got?"

"Well, like I said, he was in Portland, Oregon, for what appears to be 16 years. He rented a house, didn't own it, was married, had a child, and left rather abruptly. According to the Human Resources department at the hospital, he didn't give two weeks' notice—he just left one day."

"So, he left in a hurry," I surmised. "What else did you find?" I asked, sensing Vincent had more to share.

"It's not so much about what I did find, Martina, but what I didn't find. No divorce records and no death records for his wife and daughter."

Well, that would explain why we and the funeral director couldn't find them.

"But you have the names of the wife and daughter?"

"Yes. Rex Michels is married to Ingrid Schmidt, and their daughter's name is Cecilia Michels."

"And did you find any records for them?"

"They all abruptly stopped... Anyone want to guess how long ago?"

Feeling a pattern emerging, I said, "15 years."

"And the winner is the one and only Martina Monroe," Vincent announced with gusto.

"So, Sidney Thomas abruptly leaves a career, for which he spent what, ten years at college? After his wife—excuse me, ex-wife—disappears, he leaves town, adopts a new identity, gets married again, leaves abruptly, and there's no sign of the wife and child. Then he starts a new identity in California with his daughter Kay."

"Pretty fishy, isn't it?"

"So, wait a minute. You mentioned *a* daughter? Only one," I clarified.

"Yes, the daughter's name is Cecilia, daughter of Ingrid and

Rex. Cecilia would be twenty-seven now. No birth records for a Kay or Katherine or Kaitlyn Michels born to the two."

"So, we don't know, or I should say, we have no proof that Kay is actually his daughter."

"Bingo! And that's why we need her and Ansel's DNA."

I let out a breath. This latest news was going to be shocking for Kay. I hoped she could handle it.

20

KAY

SITTING NEXT to Becky on the sofa, I leaned over her shoulder as she tried, once again, to log into my dad's computer. Without any luck, I sighed. "Maybe we should just give up."

"Give up now? Maybe there's other ways to get into it. Like, maybe if we knew somebody who's really good at computers, they could help," Becky suggested, her determination not waning.

"Or maybe somebody at the firm where Martina and Vincent work will know what to do. As it is, Martina said she's going to come over to the house and help me look through Dad's things, hopefully uncover some evidence that will help us figure out who he was, where he's been, and what happened to my mom and my sister."

"Is it gonna be really expensive?" Becky asked.

My thoughts drifted to the stash of money I had found hidden by my dad. It was a substantial amount, but the exact cost of our ongoing investigation remained unclear. The firm had outlined their initial fees and promised an estimate of expenses after a week. I realized I should probably check in with Martina about the cost, yet I felt somewhat reassured, believing the expenses wouldn't surpass the sum I had discovered in Dad's hiding spot. Moreover, he must have had additional funds in his bank accounts... if only I could access them.

Would simply bringing his death certificate and my birth certificate be enough to prove I was his daughter? The unsettling thought lingered, especially since Martina had hinted that the document might be forged, casting doubt on the legitimacy of my entire existence.

What were my earliest memories of my dad? I strained to remember my younger years, which were hazy at best. I recalled being six, playing with Sissy, but anything before that was a blur. Perhaps that's why I couldn't recall any name changes, though Martina and Vincent insisted it must have happened at least once, alongside Dad's own identity shifts.

"I could check with them. I'm supposed to meet Martina in ten minutes. Do you want to come with me?"

"Sure," Becky replied without hesitation. Her readiness to stand by me was comforting. Martina seemed nice but we'd only just met.

"I need to figure this out before I go back to work tomorrow." My boss had been more than generous with my bereavement leave.

"Do you feel ready?"

"I guess. They told me I could take as long as I need. But it's been over a week. I plan to go back tomorrow, just to have a bit of normalcy." Returning to my job in communications at a local law firm seemed like a much-needed distraction. Between trying to uncover secrets with Becky and the official investigation led by Martina and Vincent, my mind was a whirlwind of theories and what-ifs. Work, with its typical task of drafting communications and organizing company announcements, promised a break from the chaos.

"It's probably a good idea. You can always go back, and if you decide you're not ready, will they give you more time off?"

"Probably. They're very understanding," I assured her, grateful for my employer's flexibility.

"That's good." She smiled. "So, we have to leave pretty soon?"

"Yep."

"Are you nervous?"

I could hear the concern in her voice. "Maybe a little. I've kind of got this sense that we're gonna learn some things soon, but I'm not sure it's going to be good news."

"Well, if it's not, you've got me," she reassured me.

"Thanks." Her support meant everything. "Should we bring the computer to Martina?" I asked.

"Good thinking." Becky nodded as we locked up my apartment, Dad's laptop securely tucked under my arm.

As we descended the steps from our second-story apartment toward the parking lot, Becky offered to drive. My nerves were frayed, not knowing what we would find at Dad's house—or what I'd need to face afterward.

Inside her sporty sedan, she turned on the radio, attempting to raise my spirits by humorously singing along and missing every note. Sensing my unease, she stopped singing and did a quick look over at me. "It'll be okay. I promise"

"Will it?" I couldn't help but wonder.

I didn't have the answers, but I knew hiding wasn't an option. With Becky by my side and Martina and Vincent delving into the investigation, all I could do was face whatever came my way, one step at a time.

As Becky drove down my childhood street, a sense of foreboding came over me. She approached my father's home, and my heart rate began to climb higher and higher. Why were there police cars with flashing lights parked in front of my house?

21

MARTINA

ONE OF THE officers who responded to the break-in was Officer Olsen, with whom I had worked a few crime scenes while I was employed by CoCo County. I had called the police as soon as I realized the home had been broken into, a fact made obvious as I approached the front door and it was slightly ajar. I did a quick peek inside and saw the home had been ransacked. I refrained from entering for two reasons: one, I lacked the authority, and two, I didn't want to disturb any potential evidence that could tell us who broke into the house.

What I hadn't expected when I called the police was for Hirsch to show up. Technically, he oversaw robbery and homicide, but I thought he made the effort because I was the one who made the call. He arrived just as I was explaining my presence at the house to Officer Olsen. I waved, and Hirsch parked.

Officer Olsen said, "So, you're working on a case here?"

"I am. I was coming here to help the daughter of the deceased, the owner of the home, go through his things to see if we could uncover some details about her family."

Hirsch waved as he approached us. "I came as soon as I

heard you had called in a potential break-in here. What's going on, Martina?"

"I just got here a few minutes ago. I was meeting my client, the one I told you about at lunch yesterday, to help go through the house to see if we could find any paperwork about her family. But when I arrived, someone had broken in. I didn't go inside. I just pushed the door a little with my elbow to peek in; it's been tossed."

"Where's your client?" he asked.

Almost as if on cue, a frantic Kay and her friend, Becky came running toward us. "What happened?" Kay asked.

I said, "It appears that somebody broke into your father's home."

"Did they take anything?" Kay asked.

"We don't know yet. I called the police to report the break-in. We didn't want to go inside and disturb any evidence. You won't get to go inside until it's cleared. But they will need you to take a look to see if there's anything taken once it's safe."

Kay nodded.

"Kay, this is Sergeant Hirsch of the CoCo County Sheriff's Department, and this is one of his team members, Officer Olsen." To Hirsch and Olsen, I said, "This is Kay Griffin, the homeowner's daughter, and this is her friend, Becky."

After short pleasantries, Hirsch explained, "Officer Olsen was first on the scene. We're waiting for backup to go in and do the search."

She looked puzzled. "Is it normal for a sergeant to come to a break-in?"

"He's a close personal friend, someone I used to work with. He knows a bit about your father's case," I clarified.

"Do you think it's related to his other identities?" she asked.

I hadn't had a chance to update Kay that we found her father's identity for the 16 years we hadn't previously accounted for or the fact that we thought we'd found her or her sister's birth certificate. It was strange we only found one, and I didn't like where it could lead.

As a couple of black-and-whites pulled up, Olsen said, "Sergeant Hirsch, I've got gloves and booties. Do you want me to go ahead now that backup has arrived, or did you want to do the honors?"

Hirsch said, "I'll go in with you."

"We've called in CSI too. They'll check for fingerprints. Based on what Martina's told us, we assume no one is living in the home."

"Nobody's living in the house," Kay said.

"Okay, we're going in." With that, Olsen and Hirsch hurried off to discuss strategy with the team.

To Kay, I said, "Can you think of any reason why somebody would break into your dad's house?"

Her eyes were wide as she stared at her family home. "At this point, you probably know better than I do. I have no idea. I had no idea who my dad was, so I don't know."

Becky took her hand, a sign of comfort. I was glad Kay had someone with her.

"We do have some developments, but maybe we can talk about that later."

She shook her head. "Can you tell me now? It seems like it's probably relevant, right?"

It most certainly was. "Okay. We were able to find the identity that your dad used after he left Washington State. After Sidney Thomas, he became Rex Michels and lived in Portland, Oregon. He was married to a woman named Ingrid, and they had a daughter named Cecilia," I revealed.

"Sissy," she whispered.

"We only found one birth certificate. It's either for you or your sister."

She scrunched up her face like she was having a difficult time processing it all. "If it was my mom and sister, does that mean you found their graves? You found where they are?" she asked, hopeful.

Here was the tricky part. "We haven't been able to locate any death records for Ingrid or Cecilia," I said, watching her reaction closely.

"I don't understand," she said, shaking her head in confusion.

"It could mean that they didn't die in Oregon. Or you are Cecilia. We're not sure yet. We weren't able to locate any records for Ingrid or Cecilia in Oregon within the last 15 years. We will search records in the surrounding states in case they passed or moved somewhere else," I explained.

"But how? Is it possible he had another identity after this Rex Michels character?"

"The records we could see for Rex Michels span about 16 years until he abandoned that identity and became Ansel Griffin."

Becky said, "You only found one child's birth certificate. What does that mean? It may not be for Kay? If it wasn't Kay's, where is Kay's birth certificate?" Clearly Becky was becoming Kay's personal detective.

This was going to be a difficult conversation, but it was something I was going to have to say outright. "We don't know. We couldn't find birth records for a Kay Michels, or Kay Griffin, or Kay Thomas with your father listed as the father or Ingrid listed as the mother."

"Where was Cecilia born?" she asked.

"Portland, Oregon," I confirmed.

"He told me I was born in Portland, Oregon. Maybe I am Cecilia," Kay said, her confusion growing.

It was possible that Kay might actually be Cecilia. The children looked alike, based on the photographs, but with slightly different features, so we assumed there really were two girls. The DNA test should tell us more. I'd broach the subject later, once the police were done checking the house since we'd like to obtain something with Ansel's DNA on it, which would likely come from the house. "We're not done with our investigation," I assured her.

Becky embraced her in a hug as she tried to process the news.

———

STARING OUT AT THE HOME, I thought whatever reason Ansel had for his multiple identities was likely tied to the break-in. His daughter's first sweep of the house didn't find any indication of a darker criminal side, but maybe she hadn't known where to look.

Hirsch emerged from the front door and pulled off his blue latex gloves. I met up with them, leaving Becky and Kay. Hirsch said, "It looks like somebody was looking for something inside. It's a mess in there. Hard to say if they found what they were looking for. One thing that stood out was it looked like there was a computer on the desk. There were cords but no computer."

From behind, Becky and Kay approached. Kay said, "No, I have it."

I hadn't realized they'd been close enough to hear. "You have it?" I asked, surprised.

She nodded and ran back to their car.

A few moments later, she was clutching a laptop as she jogged back toward us. "We took it to see if we could get past the password. We couldn't, so we brought it here, thinking maybe someone at your firm could get into it. Maybe that's where all his information is. Maybe he did everything online—paperless statements, that kind of thing."

Thank goodness. "My firm can absolutely look into it. We have some of the best techs in the world working for us."

"Anything else of value in the house?" Hirsch asked.

Kay said, "Not that I know of. We were here to see if we could find something useful to learn more about my dad."

"We'd like to walk you through the house so you can tell us if anything is missing or out of place. Is that okay?"

"Can my friend come with me?" she asked.

"Of course. But be warned, it's a mess in there."

Hirsch and I escorted the two women inside. We stood back and watched as Kay studied the kitchen. I leaned over and said, under my breath, "Couldn't get rid of me," giving Hirsch a knowing smile and a nudge with my elbow.

They returned, shaking their heads. "Doesn't look like anybody took anything out of the kitchen. They just went through all the drawers and the cabinets," Kay reported.

We continued throughout the house, and it was a similar story. We didn't see anything missing in any of the rooms, closets, or bathrooms. The television was where it was before, the phone was sitting on a desk, and artwork remained on the walls.

Once we were done walking through the home, we went back over to Officer Olsen and explained that nothing seemed to be missing. "Okay, well, the techs are here. They'll go ahead and do fingerprint analysis on the door. That's most likely where we will find something."

If this was a professional job, they would've worn gloves; there wouldn't be any prints. Considering how much they had tossed the home—every drawer and cabinet door was left open—they likely hadn't found what they were looking for, which I believed was most likely the laptop clutched in Kay's hands.

After wrapping things up with the officers, I told Kay not to worry, that we would get to the bottom of this and hopefully unlock the computer to find out what Griffin had been hiding. It was a stressful night, and I didn't have the heart to ask for her DNA at that point.

Once we unlocked the computer, I would have her come down to our offices, or I could go to her apartment to get a cheek swab and get DNA for Ansel from an item in the house.

Once I knew that Kay was safe with her friend, we said our goodbyes.

We'd have to return another day to help clean up the house and search for more information, but whoever broke in did half the job for us. They hadn't found anything interesting, and I didn't see any important papers anywhere. Of course, we would check the floorboards and other hidden spots. But I could feel we were one step closer to understanding Ansel Griffin's need for three identities and what happened to his two wives and his other daughter.

22

LIA

WITH MY MOM and dad at work, I spent my day in the garage, rifling through old boxes. I was on a quest to find any hint of my so-called imaginary friend. After four years of studying medicine, including the intricacies of the brain, I was well aware that our minds could play tricks on us. It was possible that this little girl, who felt as real to me as the car parked in the driveway, could have been a figment of my imagination. Yet, something deep within me—my intuition, my being—insisted that I had to find this girl, someone I had always referred to as my sister in my mind. But after countless hours with no luck, doubt began to creep in. Were these merely false memories, fabrications by my younger self's imagination?

If that were the case, it seemed cruel. Yet, the absence of any evidence of a sister—no photographs, no memories for anyone but me—led me to consider that perhaps I had concocted her existence.

Why else would my family insist she was an imaginary friend? They even smiled fondly when recalling those times I would speak of her. I didn't think they would lie to me. What motive could they possibly have? They had always been the epitome of loving parents and grandparents, offering unwavering protection, love, and support at every stage of my life.

Whenever I brought her up, I thought I detected a moment's hesitation before they would launch into their endearing stories of my childhood and longing for a sister. I had no reason to doubt them, but something niggled at my gut. Why couldn't I let it go?

Driven by a mix of desperation and determination, I began searching online for private investigators. Could they help? The thought of approaching one with my story seemed absurd—I could almost hear them laughing me out of their office. But maybe they could ask the questions that would unlock more memories, shedding light on her disappearance from my life or poking holes in my memories and finally getting me to say it was time to accept the truth.

Decision made, I resolved to hire a private investigator. If my family wouldn't or couldn't provide useful information and no records existed in our home, then this was the next logical step.

Brushing the dust off my hands onto my jeans, I headed toward the garage door to go back inside, only to be surprised by my father's presence.

"Oh, hi, Dad."

"What were you doing out here?"

"Oh, just looking for my old yearbooks," I replied, a fib slipping out.

He cocked his head, puzzled. "Aren't they in your bedroom?"

I had never lied to my father—or at least, not since I was a child trying to avoid trouble. But here I was, lying again. Why? "My high school yearbooks are there, but I was looking for my elementary school ones. I can't seem to find them."

He hesitated, then suggested, "Maybe they got lost in a move."

"Maybe," I said, hoping he didn't ask any more questions about what I was up to. "Are you off work today?" I asked, changing the subject.

"Oh no, just taking a break. I'm leaving soon for a pick-up."

My dad, a US Marshal, was the picture of strength and protection, always there for Mom and me. But he never saw women as beneath him. He and Mom were equals, partners in every sense. Their relationship was something I aspired to have myself. Mom often said that sometimes you don't get it right the first time, but when you do, it's incredible. It was in that moment that I realized the key to finding my sister.

23

MARTINA

THE SIGHT of a bouquet of yellow roses in a crystal vase on my desk took me by surprise. Who could they be from? I'd never received flowers in my entire life. It seemed unlikely that just anyone could have walked in off the street and placed them there; they must have passed through reception. Curiosity piqued, I leaned in closer, inhaling their fragrant scent. In the bunch was a plastic stick holding a note addressed to me. With a mix of anticipation and nervousness, I opened the envelope and slid out the card nestled within.

My heart skipped a beat upon reading the sender's name. They were from Charlie.

The message read,

> Dear Martina,
> Yellow roses for our friendship, that I cherish so much. Looking forward to next week.
> Love, Charlie

I was stunned by the gesture, yet hesitant to speculate on its deeper meaning. We were just friends, after all. Maybe he was thanking me for our year of friendship. That was probably all it was, right? My thoughts were abruptly interrupted by a knock on my door. "Nice flowers. Who are they from?" Vincent asked, peeking in.

"They're from my friend Charlie," I said, trying to sound nonchalant.

Vincent, with a knowing look, placed his fist on his hip. "You know, I don't recall ever sending one of my female friends flowers," he remarked, a twinkle in his eye.

His insinuation was spot on. There was indeed something special brewing between Charlie and me, and I couldn't help but look forward to what the next week would bring. "Well, everybody's different," I said, attempting to sound casual.

"And what does the card say? Considering it's from your 'friend,' it's probably not that personal, right?" he pressed.

"It is personal, Vincent," I admitted, unable to hide a smile at his persistence.

He grinned, clearly amused. "That's what I thought."

Changing the subject, I asked, "What's up?"

"Other than love in the air, just wanted to give you an update on the computer. The team says that whoever secured it didn't want anybody getting inside without their password and encryption key."

Not entirely surprising. "Any luck hacking it?"

Vincent shook his head. "Not yet. They say it could take a couple of days to extract the data off the hard drive. The normal methods of bypassing the password aren't working. It's a big job, and they wanted me to double-check if you're sure this is the direction you want to go. It can get expensive."

"We're getting inside that computer," I declared.

He nodded. "I figured, but since you're the boss, I had to get your approval."

"Full approval. In the meantime, I'll give Kay a call, have a discussion with her about what we've already found, and get her and her father's DNA."

"Good idea. Honestly, the techs were amazed by the security on this system. DNA results may come back before we crack the computer."

"Now I really want to know what's on it."

"No kidding."

Our conversation then shifted to another pressing matter. "Has Jerilyn found any new information on the Sidney Thomas identity?"

"Not sure. Haven't checked in with her. I haven't talked to her since yesterday, so maybe she's found something interesting. Let's go talk to her."

On our way to Jerilyn's cubicle, my phone vibrated in my pocket. It was a call from Charlie. Answering, I couldn't hide my excitement. "Hello?"

"Hey, Martina, just calling to say hi and see how you're doing." Charlie's voice came through, warm and comforting.

"I got the flowers. I love them, thank you," I gushed, my heart fluttering at the gesture.

"I'm glad to hear that. Only ten more days," he reminded me, referring to our upcoming date.

"Ten more days," I echoed, the anticipation building inside me.

"I'll let you go. Just wanted you to know I'm thinking of you," he said, sending my heart into a whirl.

"I'll talk to you later," I managed, barely containing my joy.

Vincent, who had been quietly observing, looked at me with wide eyes.

"What?" I asked.

"Nothing. I have nothing to say," he declared, feigning innocence.

Thankfully, the conversation ended when we arrived at Jerilyn's cubicle. "Hi."

Jerilyn said, "I'm guessing you'd like an update on Sidney Thomas?"

I nodded.

"I was just about to come find you. I think I found something kind of interesting. The marriage certificate for Sidney and Sinead came in. Neither of their parents, listed on the certificate, are still alive, but a few distant relatives are."

"How distant?" I asked.

"One's Sidney's uncle who lives in California," Jerilyn revealed.

"And he's still alive?" I pressed, sensing a potential lead.

"He's living in the Bay Area," she confirmed, which struck me as peculiar, especially since Kay had insisted she had no living relatives.

"What city?"

"You ready for this?" Jerilyn paused. "Pleasant Hill."

The same town where Ansel and Kay moved to 15 years ago? The coincidence was too stark to ignore. I needed to speak with this uncle. "How close to the Griffin house does he live?"

"Other side of town, in a care facility. But that can't be a coincidence, right?" Jerilyn asked.

"No, it couldn't," I agreed, my mind racing with the implications. "How old is the uncle?"

"Just turned 87. He was the youngest of his siblings."

Glancing at Vincent, I said, "I'd certainly like to talk to him."

"Let me print out the details for you," Jerilyn offered.

"Thank you." I said to Vincent, "You want to go interview him with me?"

"Sure. Whenever you're ready."

After a quick look at my watch, I said, "It's a little late. Let's go first thing tomorrow. I need to go talk to Kay and get a DNA sample."

"Cool."

The revelation that Kay had a relative living so close to her made me wonder if she'd known or if it was another secret her father had kept. Ansel had to have known. The question was, did he have a relationship with the uncle, and did he know what Ansel had been hiding from?

24

KAY

The police had finished collecting evidence from the break-in at my dad's house. They apologized for the mess but also explained it wasn't their responsibility to clean it up. Becky and Martina had offered to come over and help me with the job. I wasn't surprised Becky would help but was shocked when Martina offered and assured me I wouldn't be billed for it but that there was some things we needed to discuss.

With Becky by my side, I went in and turned on every single light in the house before securing the lock on the front door. In the living room, I stared out at the wreckage. Becky said, "Maybe we should get some boxes to pack things up."

It was a good suggestion. Martina and her team confirmed my father owned the home and found his bank accounts. But what did that mean for me? Could I sell the house? Live in it? Did I want to?

Probably not. It would be too strange. Or maybe it was too soon to decide. But packing up all of Dad's things was necessary for any of the situations.

A knock on the door startled me out of my thoughts.

Approaching the front door, I peered through the peephole

to see Martina standing outside. Upon me opening the door, she stepped inside. "Hi, Kay. Hi, Becky."

"Come on in," I said, closing the door behind her.

Martina said, "How are you holding up?"

"I'm okay. Feeling a little out of sorts with everything," I admitted.

Martina's expression grew concerned. "Is there anything I can do to help?"

"Well, Becky and I came to clean up the house, but she suggested perhaps I should start boxing things up. I'm just not sure what to do. Am I supposed to sell my dad's house? Is there something about inheritance? I don't know how to handle his belongings legally."

She led us back into the dining room and sat us down and said, "We're currently conducting a background check on your father's aliases. Once we can definitively prove you're his only living relative or next of kin, we'll be able to assist you with his belongings, finances, and the next steps."

Her wording puzzled me. "If I'm his daughter, why mention 'if I'm next of kin'?"

"As I mentioned, we're still finalizing the background checks. We've found a birth certificate for a child, but we need to be sure it's you. It's possible there's a missing birth certificate for you or your sister. We would like to collect some DNA from you, along with something of your father's, like a hairbrush or toothbrush, to compare and confirm your relation."

I had been wondering if they would ask for a DNA sample, but with the break-in and dealing with that, I hadn't asked about it. "Will that prove the birth certificate belongs to me?"

"It won't directly, but it will help us determine if you are his biological daughter."

"Is there something you're not telling me?"

"The initial search for Cecilia and Ingrid came up empty

when your father left Oregon and became Ansel Griffin in California. Which means another missing wife, and maybe a child, if you're not Cecilia."

This news left me trying to recall my last memories of Sissy but nothing gave me any answers. Maybe Ingrid wasn't my mother, and I wasn't Cecilia. "Were you able to find the address where he was living in Oregon?"

She nodded affirmatively.

"Do you think I should go there to see if it will jog any memories?"

"You could, but at this point, it might be wiser to stay put. We can have your DNA tested to verify your relationship, which might also aid in proving your claim to his estate. As much as you've managed with a forged document all your life, it might not suffice for the IRS."

"His toothbrush should still be in the bathroom; I can check."

"Good. Also, our technical team is still attempting to access his laptop. It's heavily secured with sophisticated encryption, making it a little more difficult to get into, but they will. It'll just take a little longer," she said.

"Is that normal? I mean, I have a laptop but nothing special, just a password."

"It's not common for the average person, but for someone owning a business or with sensitive information they wish to keep private, it's not that uncommon."

What was my dad hiding? I didn't think he had his own business, but I knew so very little about him. So, who knows? "How long do you think it will take to gain access?"

"They mentioned it could take awhile. We're calling in reinforcements, given the sophistication of the encryption. We're hopeful, though."

Feeling uneasy, I stood up. "I'll go get his toothbrush."

Reflecting on the years spent in that house, which always felt quiet and lonely, I realized I had always preferred visiting friends' homes, where the atmosphere was warm and welcoming, complete with parents and siblings—such a stark contrast to our bare and quiet home.

Ascending the stairs to my father's room, I found his toothbrush still in the cup next to the sink. I quickly placed it in a plastic bag from the kitchen and presented it to Martina. "What do you need from me?"

"I have a kit to collect your DNA from your cheek," she explained.

Nodding, I watched as she pulled out the packet from her backpack. A strange calm overtook me as I opened my mouth for the swab, feeling like answers were on the horizon—answers to questions I hadn't realized I had. If he wasn't my dad, who was my real dad?

25

MARTINA

With no further progress into Ansel's computer and the lab processing Kay and his DNA, Vincent and I headed over to the care home where Ansel's, a.k.a. Sidney Thomas's, uncle was living. Inside, I smiled and said, "Hi, we're here to visit Camden Thomas."

The receptionist, clad in light blue scrubs and sporting a name tag that read, "Tracy," greeted us with a questioning look. "Are you on the visitor's list?"

Vincent and I exchanged glances before I replied, "No, but I'm here on behalf of his nephew. Unfortunately, Camden's nephew recently passed away, and we don't think he's been notified. Camden is the only living relative we've been able to find."

"Oh, dear, that should be okay," she responded, her expression softening. She glanced down at her computer, making a note and tapping away at the keys.

"Would it be possible to see who else has visited Camden?" I asked.

"That's not usually allowed, but Camden doesn't get very many visitors, really just the one," she disclosed.

"His nephew?" I asked.

She nodded, her glasses balancing on the bottom of her nose.

"What name did he provide?"

The woman looked perplexed.

I explained, "We've recently learned that Camden's nephew went by a few different names. His birth name was Sidney Thomas, but in the end, he went by a different name."

Tracy said, "Ansel Griffin."

"That's one of his aliases."

"It's not his real name?" she asked, her eyebrows raised in surprise.

I shook my head. "It's not."

"Oh my."

"If you don't mind us asking, how is Camden? I've read that he's 87 years old. Is he of sound mind?" I asked.

The nurse nodded. "He has his good days and his bad days. He's mostly lucid, but his memory comes and goes. He seems to always remember Ansel and always enjoys the visits."

That answered our questions about whether or not Camden had been in touch with his nephew and vice versa. "How's his health?"

"I'm really not supposed to say, but since Ansel is his only living relative, I guess it's okay. He has lung cancer. They don't think he'll live much longer."

"I'm sorry to hear that. What's he like, his demeanor?"

"He's a bit salty, I guess you could say. Off the record, though, right?" she whispered, leaning closer.

"Yes, we're just investigators looking into family matters," I assured her.

"Oh, okay. Well, yeah, he's not a favorite of the staff. He kind of stares a lot, which isn't unusual with patients here, but...

Yeah, there's just something about him. Between you and me, he's kind of a creep," she confided.

A family trait? "We'd like to speak to him, if that's okay," I said, bringing the conversation back to our purpose.

"Of course," she replied, glancing around before hurrying us down the hall. "I'm not supposed to leave the desk, but I'll go with you to let him know you're here," she whispered as she led us to the door.

She knocked before opening it slightly. "Mr. Thomas, you have some visitors."

"Who is it?" a voice called from within.

"Friends of your nephew. Can they come in?"

He didn't answer. Tracy gave us a look, shrugged, and hurried back to the front desk, leaving us to introduce ourselves.

I stepped inside, with Vincent trailing behind me. "Mr. Thomas, my name is Martina Monroe, and this is my partner, Vincent Teller. We have a few questions about your nephew, Ansel."

"I don't know nothing about Ansel," he said gruffly.

"The reason we're here to talk about Ansel is that I'm afraid we have some bad news," I continued, noticing his gaze shift back to me.

His eyes were milky and twitchy. "Oh."

"Ansel passed away nearly two weeks ago. We would've come by to tell you earlier, but his daughter was told he didn't have any living relatives."

Camden looked away.

"But we know he had relatives, and we know that his name was Sidney Thomas before he changed it a few times."

"I don't know anything about what Sid did."

Vincent shot me a look and smirked. "With all due respect, you obviously know something about it. You called him Ansel, yet you know that's not his real name."

"Oh, you're a sharp one, aren't you?" Camden's voice dripped with venom.

"We'd just like to understand more about Ansel and his life. He has a daughter; have you met her?"

"I don't know nothing," he insisted.

"We're looking for any other relatives of Sidney's. We're having a difficult time finding them, even though we know he's been married twice."

"I told you I don't know nothing about nothing."

"He's dead. You don't have to protect him anymore."

Camden laughed, a sound that sent a shiver down my spine. Missing a few teeth and looking worse for wear, he seemed to be consumed by his illness. "They'll never get me," he declared, turning his attention back to the window.

I glanced over at Vincent, his eyebrows raised.

"What do you know about Ansel and Kay? Where is her mother?"

Silence enveloped the room.

Shaking my head, I had a sinking feeling that whatever Ansel, Sidney, or Rex was involved in, his uncle Camden knew all about it. Perhaps what had drawn him to the Bay Area was, in fact, Camden Thomas.

Time to pull out the big guns. "You can stay silent, but there isn't much we won't learn on our own. We have his DNA and his daughter's being processed to see if she is his daughter. Not to mention we have Ansel's computer. Technicians are unlocking the encryption as we speak." Not entirely true, but they had copied the hard drive and were working around the clock to access the system without triggering any kind of shut-down or erase program.

Camden flinched.

"That's right. Whatever he was hiding, or you are, will soon be brought to light," I stated firmly.

He turned once again, staring directly into my eyes. He wheezed and then said, "I'd like you to leave."

"Gladly. We'll go. It was nice meeting you, Camden. I have a feeling we'll be seeing each other again," I said, signaling to Vincent that it was time to go.

26

MARTINA

BRIGHT AND EARLY MONDAY MORNING, we received the heartbreaking news. I should have known the weekend was too quiet and peaceful for that vibe to last.

What began as a young woman wanting to know where her mother and her sister were buried, so she could bury her father right next to them—an act of love and compassion—had resulted in Kay's whole world being turned upside down. All leading to more questions than answers. And I was about to deliver some answers that I didn't think she'd ever had questions for.

My gut had told me this was a possibility. I had warned Kay to bring a friend to our meeting—she was going to need a lot of support in that moment, more than ever before. And my heart truly broke for her and the lives that had been destroyed.

"Thank you for coming in, Kay. And it's good to see you again, Becky. You're a good friend," I began.

She smiled and said, "I brought fudge for both of you. You've been such a big help. Seems like it was outside of your job description to help pack up the house. It's really kind of you."

It was difficult to be upbeat at a time like this, but I didn't want to seem ungrateful. "Thank you, that's very nice. I look forward to it. I'll even share with my daughter if she's home."

Kay looked at me, surprised. "You have a daughter?"

"I do. She's nineteen and is on summer break after her first year at UC Davis."

"With you as a mom, I bet she has stories," Becky said with a smile.

"You don't have a mom who is a private investigator without having a few stories," I said, but I didn't want to prolong the news much longer. "Like I told you on the phone, there have been additional developments in the case."

Kay reached for her friend's hand and squeezed. Perhaps Kay had been preparing herself for another bombshell.

"As I told you last week, we believe that Ansel Griffin, also known as Sidney Thomas, was from Redmond, Washington. He had been married to a woman named Sinead. Sinead went missing the same year he left Washington and became Rex Michels. As Rex Michels, he married a woman named Ingrid and had a child named Cecilia. When we did a background check for his first wife, Sinead, we found that she's been listed in a missing person database. As for his second wife and daughter, we've searched for records for them, but they seemingly disappeared when he became Ansel Griffin and moved to California from Portland, Oregon." I waited for nods to show they were up to speed. "We were recently able to locate a family member—his name is Camden Thomas, and he lives in Pleasant Hill. He is Ansel's, or rather Sidney's uncle, 87 years old, and is currently in a nursing home. Ansel was a regular visitor, his only visitor, actually. We notified him of his nephew's death."

Kay shook her head in disbelief. "I have family living in Pleasant Hill? Are you kidding?"

"I'm afraid not, but there's more," I said, my voice somber, Vincent quiet as well. The look on Kay and Becky's faces showed they knew what I was about to tell Kay would change everything.

"We spoke with him and he didn't give us any information."

"Did he know about me?"

"He wouldn't tell us anything about Ansel or his family."

"That's weird, right?" Becky asked.

"It's unusual."

"Is that it? I have a relative?"

Time to rip off the Band-Aid. "No. That's not all. The lab came back with the DNA results for the comparison between the toothbrush from Ansel and your cheek swab. Based on the analysis, Ansel was not your father."

Her eyes flew wide open. "He's not my dad? How can that be?" As she sat in disbelief, tears streamed down her face as Becky held her.

The lab results came back on Saturday evening, but Vincent, ever diligent, knew that we had to look into Kay's background further before meeting with her and telling her the news.

We both suspected something was very wrong from the moment we met her, and her story about her odd childhood, the father who wouldn't speak of their past, and the lack of photographs of her—not to mention a secret life and a computer that had taken nearly five days to crack. The lab was still working on it, saying they were close. One could only imagine what we'd find on that computer.

Vincent offered tissues.

Once calm, Kay looked at the two of us, "And you're sure? You're really sure?"

"Yes. There's more." I glanced at Becky to convey that Kay needed her support now more than ever.

Vincent took over to explain what else he found. "Yes, like Martina said, there's more. When I received the results from the lab confirming Ansel is not your biological father, I did some additional digging. I utilized facial recognition technology in a somewhat unique way, trying to predict what you might have looked like as a child. From there I searched NamUs, that is the National Missing and Unidentified Persons System, a national database for missing and exploited children. Based on the search, you might be one of the missing children. There is one in particular from Ashland, Oregon who is a striking resemblance. We won't be able to confirm until we speak to law enforcement and can submit your DNA for analysis."

When Vincent told me this, I reached out to Hirsch, but he said it would be better to go through the Ashland Police Department, where the girl was reported missing. Hirsch promised to put in a good word to get the job done quickly.

I said, "I know this is a lot to take in."

Kay sat stunned. Becky looked at me and said, "Kay was kidnapped as a young girl and was raised by Ansel who pretended to be her dad?"

"It appears that way."

"Have you found her parents?"

Before I could answer, Kay said, "Can I see? The picture of the girl you think is me?"

Vincent opened up his laptop and pulled up the photo. He turned the monitor to face Kay and Becky.

Kay's face fell as she studied the photo and read the details for the little girl, Kaitlyn Ramsey's, disappearance.

Kaitlyn Ramsey's parents, Dana and Tom, reported her missing 21 years ago when she was just four years old. Dana and Kaitlyn were at a shopping mall, in a toy store. Dana said she only turned around for a minute, but when she looked back, Kaitlyn was gone. She immediately reported her missing to store security, and the mall security was alerted too, but it was too late.

"It looks like me. I ... think it is me." Kay began heaving, overwhelmed by the news.

"Just breathe in and out," I encouraged her, waiting in silence until her breathing evened out.

"We'll need to compare DNA to be sure."

Becky said, "How long will that take?"

"It could be a few days or a week. We have to work with the Ashland Police Department to compare Kay's DNA to the sample submitted by the Ramseys. I know this is a tremendous amount of information," I said. "Kay, I've called a friend of mine, a counselor, if you'd like to speak with her. She can be here in twenty minutes. She specializes in these types of cases. It could really help."

She sat there looking into the corner of the room, her gaze distant. Perhaps memories, or pieces of her childhood, were being pieced back together with this shocking realization.

"What about my sister? Or the girl. Sissy. What if she was taken too?"

It was a scenario I had considered, fitting with her description of her sister—hiding from monsters, there one day and inexplicably gone the next, with a parental figure telling her she couldn't ask questions about it. "It's possible," I acknowledged.

She shook her head, but then a spark of recollection lit her eyes. "But the photo album... She's in the photo album. Whoever she is—the little girl from my memories. She's in that photo album. She must be Cecilia, his actual daughter. What happened to her? Can we find out?"

The girl she once believed to be her sister might have held a significance beyond her understanding. At four years old, she had likely been kidnapped, and perhaps "Sissy" had been a lifeline that got her through the harrowing adjustment period. Only she knew how daunting and terrifying those moments had been, making "Sissy" her beacon of hope during such a dark time.

"Do you still want us to locate her?" I asked.

Regardless of her answer, I wouldn't stop until I found her. This was not a mission one could simply abandon. If my hunch about Griffin was correct—that he was indeed a malevolent figure—he may have been involved in more kidnappings. The victims and their families deserved answers.

"Yes, I feel it's really important," she confessed, her voice trembling with a mixture of fear and resolve. "I can't explain it, but I feel this deep connection to her. Is that crazy?"

"It's not."

"And if I'm Kaitlyn—" She paused, as if the name was suddenly familiar. "What about my parents? Are they still alive? Are they looking for me?"

"They are still alive and looking for Kaitlyn. But we need to get the DNA results back before we contact them." I didn't want to get their hopes up, if it wasn't her. It would be devastating to them if they for a moment thought their daughter was alive and then a terrible blow if she wasn't.

"Okay," she agreed, the determination in her eyes unmistakable. Turning to her friend Becky, she said with a shaking voice, "I was kidnapped. He wasn't my dad."

Becky nodded, squeezing her hand in silent solidarity. "I'm here for you, anything you need."

27

KAY

Back inside my apartment, I paced back and forth on the living room floor contemplating everything I'd just learned. Becky sat quietly, her eyes following my every move, a concerned look etched on her face. The realization had hit me like a tidal wave. I said, "My whole life has been a lie." Shaking my head in disbelief, I continued, "I was kidnapped when I was little. Why don't I remember? If I was taken when I was four years old, I guess I wouldn't remember anything before that. But Sissy... I remembered Sissy. She was my earliest memory. She was there, hiding from monsters."

Becky remained silent.

A shiver ran through me as the pieces started to align, an ominous feeling revealing the truth. "Oh my gosh, my dad was the monster. But there were more monsters. She didn't say 'the monster.' She said 'monsters.' What did they do to Sissy? I don't remember any monsters. If I wasn't hurt like her, why was I taken?"

I paused, the room suddenly feeling smaller. "Dad was strict and weird about so many things. Dad... he wasn't my dad."

Becky's voice, soft and filled with concern, broke through my spiraling thoughts. "Are you OK? Can I get you anything?"

"OK? I don't think so. I don't even know my name, who my parents were, or where I was really born. I don't know anything." The weight of the questions pressed down on me. It was too much to process, but at the same time I needed more information. I needed to know why. Why did he take me? I didn't remember any sexual abuse or having weird photos taken of me.

My thoughts turned to Sissy. What really happened to Sissy? Did she die, or was she a kidnapped little girl whose family found her? Or did he kill her, or did he sell her to a monster? I had read about the horrors of human trafficking and feared that was what happened to Sissy.

Another thought popped into my mind. Did I have siblings? Ansel wasn't my father, and my parents, they could've had more children. I could have actual siblings. The thought of Sissy being my sister felt so real, yet it was likely she wasn't my actual sister, I understood that now. It was unlikely he took two girls from the same family. There was a photo album. It had to be his other daughter, his only daughter from his second wife, the one Martina and Vincent couldn't find.

I needed answers, yet one question echoed louder than the rest. The thoughts swirled and twirled, and I couldn't stop from asking why. Why had he taken me?

Becky's voice once again cut through my thoughts, tinged with worry. "You're beginning to worry me."

Looking at her, a resolve settled over me. "I think I know what I have to do."

"What do you have to do?" Becky asked.

"I'm going to talk to his uncle. Martina said he's in a nursing home in Pleasant Hill. There aren't many, probably. I don't really know, but we do know his name—Camden Thomas.

Technically, according to my documents, I'm his niece. Anyway, he has to have answers. Ansel had been in contact with him. He must know about me. He has to have answers, right?"

Becky slowly lifted herself off the couch and walked toward me. "I'm not sure that's a great idea."

"Why not? He might have answers. He knew my dad...but not my dad. I need to talk to him. I want answers. I want to know about him. I want to know why I was taken, why this person who I thought was my dad would rip me away from my real family just to make me someone new."

My body shook as the emotional turmoil within me surged and the tears streamed down my face. Becky wrapped her arms around me, comforting me as I cried, trying to make sense of everything that was happening in my life. After a moment, I gently removed her arms and asked, "Will you go with me to see Camden?"

"Maybe you should talk to Martina and Vincent first. They said this Camden person wouldn't talk to them. I think you should wait until Martina and Vincent find answers," she suggested, caution in her voice.

"What, so they can tell me not to talk to him? That it's dangerous? Guess what—my dad's...not my dad. Why do I keep saying that? He's not my dad." My words were shaky, over-whelmed by too much all at once.

Becky said, "Maybe we should have a good sleep tonight and think about it, OK?"

"How can I sleep knowing my whole life has been a lie?" I countered, my resolve hardening. I shook my head, wiping the tears from my face with the back of my sleeve. "No, I'm going there tonight, and I'm getting answers, one way or another."

28

MARTINA

WHAT A DAY IT HAD BEEN. I couldn't help but feel a profound sense of empathy for Kay, although she had steadfastly refused to speak with a counselor. Perhaps, after she returned home and had some time to process the avalanche of revelations about her family—or rather, her non-family, as it turned out—she might reconsider. It was going to take several days to confirm if she was indeed Kaitlyn Ramsey. I found myself hoping she was. Kay's composite was a remarkably close match to the little girl kidnapped at the age of four. It seemed highly likely it was her, especially considering where Ansel had been at the time of her disappearance in Oregon, the very state from which she had been snatched. He could very well be the kidnapper, and she could be Kaitlyn Ramsey.

Our next steps were clear: compare her DNA to that of Kaitlyn Ramsey. This would not only bring her answers but might also reunite her with her family, if they were still searching for her. Since our meeting, I had already taken to the internet, scouring for any information on Kaitlyn Ramsey's family, wondering if they were still in Oregon or if they had other children.

My search led me to a Facebook page dedicated to finding Kaitlyn. The family had posted pictures and age-progressed images of what Kaitlyn might look like now. The resemblance to Kay was remarkable. It had to be her.

The determination of her family was palpable in each post. They had never given up, evidenced by family photos and one particularly heart-wrenching image of a mom, dad, and a little boy with a caption that pleaded, "Please bring our Kaitlyn home."

If Kay was indeed Kaitlyn, it appeared she had a little brother. While I wasn't the biggest proponent of this burgeoning social media phenomenon, its growing popularity was undeniable. Platforms like these allowed individuals like Kaitlyn's family to share their stories with potentially hundreds of thousands, if not millions, of people. Perhaps one day, these digital networks could play a pivotal role in solving crimes, if they hadn't already. It struck me that many of the cases that were solved, especially the tough ones, were due to the relentless determination of the families involved. Kaitlyn's case might just be the next one to join those ranks.

I hoped Ashland PD would be able to compare Kay's and Kaitlyn's DNA soon, finally bringing answers for her, and hopefully reunite Kay with her family.

A sudden eruption of loud yelling and cheers pierced the usual calm of the office, breaking my concentration. It wasn't typical for our team to be so boisterous, especially not without a good reason. I left my office and ventured down the hallway, the sounds of celebration growing louder with each step. The cacophony of high-fives and jubilant shouting led me directly to the tech cave, the epicenter of the commotion.

"What's going on?" I asked, stepping into the room filled with an electric energy.

Vincent, hunched over a monitor alongside Lewis, one of

our computer geniuses, looked up with a grin spreading across his face. "We're in, Martina."

"Ansel Griffin's computer?" I asked, a mix of surprise and anticipation building within me.

He nodded. "Looks like there's tons of data to sift through, but we got in. Not me, of course, but the team—Lewis, mostly."

Lewis had been with the firm a few years—a former FBI agent with a penchant for computer wizardry. His expertise was invaluable, and today, it seemed, he had outdone himself. "Well done, Lewis. When do you think we'll get anything usable off of it?"

"If I down a couple of Red Bulls, I could keep going. See what I find," he said, a determined glint in his eye.

"You don't have to work all night," I said, sensing the intense focus in the room. The team's dedication was clear, yet the sudden silence caught me off guard. "What?" I asked, confused by their reaction.

Lewis's expression turned serious. "Martina, anybody who put this level of encryption on their computer is doing seriously bad things. And you said he may be a kidnapping suspect. This could be huge."

It was a good point. "I'll go get you that Red Bull," I said with a supportive smile, turning to leave as Vincent tagged along.

"Sounds like we're gonna find out what's up with this guy after all," Vincent said with a hint of optimism.

"Yeah, and if we could find his wife and child, maybe they can answer some questions too."

"I feel like Kay deserves that. She had that special bond with Sissy. It's probably his daughter, Cecilia, the one who disappeared with the second wife. You think they're still out there?"

"I have no idea, Vincent. This case has been a roller coaster. All we can do is hope for the best."

Now, with a breakthrough within our grasp, the urgency to uncover what was hidden on that darn computer was more pressing than ever. It was time to understand why Sidney a.k.a. Rex a.k.a. Ansel had changed identities and had kidnapped Kay.

29

LIA

Sitting in front of the television, immersed in an episode of "Friends," I found myself lost in thought, reflecting on my earlier meeting with the private investigator. As I had anticipated, there wasn't much to go on, yet I had provided some generic information for the PI to start digging into my past, into who we were before we moved in with Grandma and Grandpa. My mom had always insisted on certain topics being off-limits, subjects we were never to discuss, and I had respected her wishes—until now.

The sound of the front door opening snapped me back to reality. Dad walked in, his usual smile absent, replaced by a stern expression that immediately set me on edge. "Hey, Dad," I said, trying to gauge his mood.

"I need to talk to you," he stated, his tone firm and devoid of its usual warmth.

His anger was obvious, and I couldn't help but wonder why. Did he know about the small lie I told him earlier, about looking for yearbooks? Was that what had upset him? I turned off the television, bracing myself for the conversation. "What is it?"

"Did you talk to a private investigator today?" he asked.

His knowledge of my meeting with the PI took me by surprise. "Yes, why?" I said, confused about why this would make him angry.

Red-faced, he said, "Why are you asking me why? I told you there are things from the past you cannot go back to."

"I just want to know if she was real, Dad," I said, voicing the question that had haunted me for years. Despite everyone's insistence that she was just an imaginary friend, I needed to know once and for all.

"What you did was really dangerous."

The family secrets had always been a mystery to me, shrouded in warnings never to delve into our past or speak of where we used to live or of my biological father. These rules were presented as protective measures, but I struggled to understand what or who we were being protected from.

I was very young when Mom met Dad. She worked at a coffee shop then, and he was a regular, always stopping by in the morning with one of his partners. She remembered his order and he remembered her smile. Their story began when he asked her out, sensing that she was hiding from something or someone, her fear palpable.

Mom eventually opened up to him about everything.

Being in the US Marshals, Dad knew how to keep her safe, teaching her strategies to stay one step ahead of whatever or whoever she was running from. They didn't explain much to me, only emphasizing the need for safety and silence about our previous lives.

As Dad stood before me now, the weight of our unspoken past heavy between us, I realized that my quest for answers might have unearthed more than just the truth about a possibly imaginary sister. It threatened the very fabric of the life we had together.

"Dad, I'm 27 years old. You don't have to protect me

anymore. I'm a grown woman. I'm a doctor, and I hold people's lives in my hands. I think I deserve to know the truth, don't you?" I pleaded, seeking the truth I felt was long overdue.

His face, a canvas of mixed emotions, softened as he took a seat next to me. The warmth of his hand enveloped mine. "You're right. You deserve to know the truth, but it's not pretty. Honestly, we thought it was better that you didn't know."

I believed him, just as I believed my mom and my grandparents—that they had always done what they thought was best for me. But the right to know the truth was something I couldn't forgo any longer. "Will you tell me the truth?"

"Let's wait for your mother to get home. I want her to tell you, okay?"

"But what if she won't tell me? She's been hiding this from me my whole life."

"I think you make a good argument. You're a grown woman now, as much as we hate to admit it. You deserve it. If she doesn't want to tell you, I'll have a talk with her."

"Thanks."

My father continued, "And the private investigator—I've told him to stop looking into anything you had him look into."

"How did you even know?" I asked, bewildered.

"A lot of private investigators are ex-law enforcement. A friend of mine saw the name and called me."

It dawned on me then that my parents' efforts to keep me safe had effectively placed me in a bubble, one I hadn't fully realized I was in until then. "Okay, if you tell me the truth, I'll stop looking for her."

He nodded slowly, pulling me into a hug. "Just remember, we did this all to keep you safe."

The embrace was a bittersweet reminder of the lengths to which my family had gone to protect me, even if it meant keeping me in the dark.

As I waited for my mom to get home, I braced myself for the answers that would soon come, wondering if the truth would change my whole world.

"Are you sure you want to do this?" Becky asked.

"I'm absolutely 100% positive, Becky. If this guy knows anything about Ansel, or whoever he is, and why he took me away from my whole life when I was four, then I wanna know." My determination might have seemed a bit intense, my eyes wide and my body thrumming with a nervous energy as we stepped into the nursing home.

Finding Camden Thomas hadn't been difficult. It only took a few phone calls to local nursing homes that led us right to him.

I flashed a convincing smile at the man in scrubs behind the reception desk. "Hi, my name is Kay, and I'm here to see my great uncle Camden," I said, trying to sound as casual as possible.

"Oh, Camden Thomas is your great uncle?" he replied, a flicker of surprise crossing his face.

"Yeah, he's my dad's uncle. My dad died recently, so I thought I would come and visit him," I lied smoothly. Although if I hadn't just learned Ansel wasn't my father, it wouldn't have been a lie.

"Okay, he should just be back from dinner. Go ahead and sign in here," he said, handing me a sign-in sheet.

I scribbled down "Kay Griffin," the only identity I knew, and followed the man down the hallway. He knocked on an open door. "Camden, you've got some more visitors," he announced.

I turned to him quickly. "Did somebody else visit him today?" Pausing to come up with the reason for wanting to know, I quickly said, "There are a lot of family in town for the memorial. I'm curious who stopped by."

He nodded, accepting my explanation, and I sighed inwardly in relief. "If I recall, it was one of Camden's nephews. I guess that would make him your uncle."

"What did he look like? I have a few."

"Dark hair, glasses, mustache, maybe in his 50s."

"Joe?" I asked.

"Oh, yeah, I think that was his name."

"Thanks."

That guy, "Joe," knew Ansel's uncle?

As we entered the room, a man sitting by the window turned his gaze toward Becky and me. There was something unsettling about the way he looked at us, something not quite right, but at that moment, my focus was solely on finding the truth.

"Are you Camden Thomas?" I asked, walking straight up to him, not breaking eye contact.

"I am. Who are you?" he responded, his voice wheezy and strained.

The moment had arrived, standing face to face with the man who could answer questions about my past. Steeling my nerves, I said, "My name is Kay Griffin. I am Ansel's daughter."

Camden Thomas shook his head dismissively. "I don't know

nothing about that," he rasped, his voice showing the toll of years or illness, or perhaps both.

"Oh, really?" I countered, inching closer despite Becky's gentle pull on my arm, urging me to maintain my distance from the man whose very presence seemed to darken the room. "I know he took me, and I know that he visited you before he died. I want to know why he took me. I'm pretty sure you know why."

"I don't know nothing about nothing, young lady," he retorted, sizing me up with a look that made my skin crawl. The way he licked his lips was repulsive, and I fought the urge to flee then and there. I caught Becky's eye; her expression was filled with concern.

"I will get to the truth, and if you're just trying to cover for him, you're going to go down too," I said, my determination hardening even as his smile—a grimace of missing and yellowed teeth—made my stomach churn. He was like a human jack-o'-lantern, hollowed out and grotesque.

"I'm looking forward to seeing you and your pretty friend again," he taunted, sending a shiver down my spine.

"Come on, let's go, Kay," Becky urged, pulling me away from the creature.

As we made our way out, I couldn't help but throw one last glance at Camden, a vow that I would uncover the truth, regardless of his silence.

Back in the hallway, the man at the desk noted our departure. "Short visit?" he asked.

"It was. What's wrong with him?" I couldn't hide the revulsion in my voice, my body still reacting to the vile energy of Camden Thomas.

"Lung cancer," he said, his voice neutral.

"He's a vile person," I couldn't help but say it out loud.

The man said, "He's nobody's favorite around here."

"Can you tell me who has visited him, other than my uncle?" I asked, hoping for a lead.

"Just a private investigator and her partner," he said.

I nodded. "I hired them to find him. Tonight was our first meeting." Part of me wished I hadn't come to talk to him. I should have listened to Becky.

Camden Thomas had left me with a serious case of the creeps, a feeling I wasn't sure I could shake off. First thing I would do when I got home was take a shower and try to scrub the ick off me.

"Well, you can check that off your list, huh?" the man said, a hint of empathy in his voice.

"Yeah, thanks," I said, exiting the nursing home with Becky by my side, both of us eager to leave the experience behind. As we stepped into the fresh air, I wondered if the stain of that encounter would ever truly fade.

31

MARTINA

Standing at Vincent's cubicle, I was filled with anticipation. "I just got a call from Lewis. He found something on Griffin's computer."

Vincent sprang from his seat. "Let's grab a Red Bull from the kitchen for him; he's been here all night."

As we hurried toward the refrigerator, I continued to be amazed by the team's dedication. With an energy drink in hand, we made our way to the tech cave, the heart of our operation, where Lewis had been piecing together fragments of Ansel's computer.

"Hey, Lewis," I said, handing over the can of Red Bull as a token of our appreciation for his tireless work.

Vincent said, "Hey, man. Martina said you found something?"

Lewis nodded, his expression grave. "Yep. Once I was able to crack the encryption, I started going through the directory. The first files I opened were images. But to fully understand what this guy was up to, I still need to go through the other files. You'll understand why in a minute."

"Is it bad?" I asked, even though I had a feeling it was.

"Let's put it this way. I wish I'd never seen any of it and hope I'll be able to remove them from my memory." The solemnity in Lewis's voice sent a chill down my spine.

Vincent and I exchanged glances, getting ourselves ready for what was to come.

I said, "All right, show me the first one."

Lewis nodded, his fingers tapping away at the keys until an image materialized on the large monitor.

My stomach flip-flopped at the sight. I studied the image and said a silent prayer for the little girl on the screen. Her eyes were closed, and I hoped she was merely sleeping and nothing worse.

Vincent said, "I'm guessing there's more."

Lewis nodded again, and with each subsequent image, my heart sank further. Another child, eyes closed, but with a healthy color—likely not deceased, but posed—unclothed. "Show me a few more," I urged, desperate to find a pattern, thinking we might find something that would point to the identity of the photographer.

As Lewis continued, a detail caught my eye. "Stop," I said, pointing to a man in one of the pictures. "That guy has a tattoo."

Lewis looked at me expectantly. "Did the owner of the laptop have a tattoo?"

That was a good question. We would check with the medical examiner. "Not sure. We'll check."

"Does this surprise you?"

"No. He's a suspect in the kidnapping of a four-year-old girl. Usually, men who do that...the reason is pretty consistent." Finding the child sexual abuse materials on Ansel's computer was what I had feared. "Any indication this is his personal collection or...for sale?"

"That's where the other files are going to come in handy," Lewis said, indicating the digital mountain we had yet to climb.

"I might need some extra hands on it to get it done faster. Vincent, you're pretty good with a computer, right?"

"Yep. Not great at encryption, but I know how to piece together files," he said.

"All right, if you need extra hands, we've got more folks around," I offered.

Lewis said, "I'll let you know if we need more help and if we find additional evidence."

"Are you going to call Hirsch?" Vincent asked.

"I will. I need to understand who has jurisdiction. This was found in Pleasant Hill, so it may be CoCo County's responsibility, but if the images were purchased or sold over state lines, they may turn it over to the FBI."

With nods, I let them get to work. As I headed toward my office to call Hirsch, the dread of informing Kay about our findings weighed on me. The images, depicting children with their eyes closed as if in slumber, hinted at a sinister truth likely involving drugging. I didn't think Kay had been immune and it could explain why she didn't have memories of the acts captured on film. Kay had already been through so much—discovering her entire life was based on a lie, learning that the man she thought was her father had kidnapped her. The added knowledge she likely had been sexually abused may be too much.

In my office, I shut the door and called Hirsch. After pleasantries, I explained our discovery and that we were still recovering files to further investigate the extent of the crime. "Is it under your jurisdiction since the laptop was retrieved in Pleasant Hill?"

"It is. I mean, obviously, it'll likely go up to the FBI, but yeah, that's awful, Martina."

It was as I thought. "I'll talk to the team and get a copy of the hard drive for CoCo County."

"Technically, you should be handing it all over, but I know you're not using it for nefarious purposes. When your team is done, I'll send folks over to retrieve all of it and put it into evidence officially."

"Okay, give me a few days."

"Faster is better."

"I'll see what I can do. I want to be able to explain all of this to Kay."

"As fast as you can is most appreciated."

"Will do, Hirsch." Hanging up, I was left to think about the terrible realities children like Kay faced, assuming we'd retrieve pictures of her on the computer. How many images would they find? How many children had been hurt? And where were they now?

Despite everything, Kay had managed to lead a seemingly normal life up to this point—a testament to her resilience. But the memories of a little girl she believed to be her sister had led her to search for her and find much more than she bargained for. It left me wanting to find the truth about Sissy and Kay's family more than ever.

32

MARTINA

Two DAYS LATER, Lewis and the team had mapped out the contents of Ansel Griffin's computer. What they uncovered was a serious criminal organization that sold child sexual abuse materials (CSAM) to anyone willing to pay. The very large sums of money transactions logged made it clear that the laptop was a smoking gun of sorts. And the individuals connected to the operation would surely want to get their hands on it. And it made me believe the computer was the object the burglar who had broken into Ansel's house was after. It gave me an uneasy feeling, compelling me to call Kay immediately.

Her phone rang, and she picked up after the third ring. "Hello."

"Hi, Kay, this is Martina. Are you at work? Is this a good time?"

"I can take a quick break. Give me a second." I heard indistinguishable movement, indicating she likely moved to a location more suitable for a private conversation.

"OK, I'm outside now. What's happening?"

"We were able to get into Ansel's computer."

"Is it bad? I know it's bad. It's bad, isn't it?"

"I'd rather not talk about the details of what we found quite yet—not over the phone. But I recall you said someone visited the house. Someone who claimed his name was Joe and that he had worked with your dad at the medical practice, but we learned that wasn't true."

"Oh, yeah, and he visited his uncle too."

He visited the uncle too? How would she know that? "Kay, how do you know that?"

Kay's initiative to seek answers on her own was unexpected, but then again, she had gone to Ansel's place of work checking up on Joe to see if he really worked in the medical office, so it wasn't out of the question. It made me realize I needed to be careful with what information I gave her.

She said, "I went to see Camden Thomas. I wanted to know why Ansel took me, but he wouldn't tell me anything. He just said that he didn't know anything and looked at me like I was... I don't know, he gave me the creeps. I told him that I wouldn't let it go, and this wasn't the last he'd heard of us."

"Who was with you?"

"Becky came with me."

At least she wasn't alone, but I still didn't like it. "What else happened? How do you know that Joe visited?"

"I asked the receptionist. He told me Camden had lots of visitors lately. So, I asked who else visited. He said it was a man named Joe matching the description of the guy who came by the house."

This "Joe" character was likely part of the organization we had discovered on the computer. "Listen to me very carefully, Kay." I paused again, reminding myself I needed to stop referring to him as her father; we knew he wasn't. "Some very bad things were discovered on Ansel's computer. These discoveries could make a lot of people very nervous. And if they think you have the computer, they could come after you. I need you to avoid going by Ansel's house and to be observant of your surroundings. If Joe comes near you, don't engage. Just leave, call the police, or call me. I'll come get you."

"Oh, okay. Should I be worried?"

Knowing that Kay and Becky were investigating on their own, I was even more concerned for Kay. The woman had already endured so much, and she could be in real danger. My gut told me Ansel's associates wouldn't stop until they found the computer. "I do. It may not be safe to stay at your apartment. Is there someone you can stay with?"

"I could ask around. Is Becky okay to stay there?"

"No. She'll need to stay with family or friends too." If the criminals came after Kay, they may not know what she looked like and do something to Becky, thinking it was Kay.

A thought struck me—Kay was a 25-year-old single woman, and her friend Becky was the same. They wouldn't be any trouble, and I had a guest room. "Actually, Kay, you and Becky can stay with me. I have an extra room. Maybe just for a night, just until we can get some of this sorted out, okay?"

"It's really that bad? And you'd be willing to let us stay at your house?"

"Only if you're comfortable. My daughter is home from college; she's 19, loves to bake, and she loves sparkles. And she's very nice. We also have a little dog who'll let us know if anybody's near our house, plus we have a state-of-the-art security system. I would really feel better if you stayed with us."

"I don't even know what to say. That's so nice of you. Do you always do this for your clients?"

"If my clients are in trouble or could be in danger, I absolutely protect them in any way I can."

"OK, I'll talk to Becky."

"Great." It made me feel better to know the two women would be safe.

"Can I ask what was on the computer?"

She had obviously caught on it was bad enough that she'd need to go into hiding. "That's a discussion to have in person, not over the phone. Why don't you and Becky meet me at my office after you get off work, and I'll explain everything?"

"OK, can I go by my apartment first, to pick up a few things?"

"If you have to. Be really quick, and then meet me at my office this afternoon, okay?"

"All right, thanks."

I hung up, feeling the weight of responsibility. I hadn't wanted to give her the news of what we found on the computer over the phone. It was horrifying, and it would undoubtedly shatter her world even further.

A knock on my door snapped me out of my focus. As I looked up, I couldn't help but welcome the sight of the person standing before me—a face I could definitely get used to seeing every day in my office. "Hey, Hirsch."

"Hey, Martina, is this a good time? I've got the team here."

I stood up. "Yes, I was just talking to Kay, letting her know that I'd feel better if she stayed with me tonight."

"Are you really that concerned?"

"If someone's looking for that computer, and they think she has it, they could go after her."

"Understood. And considering my team hasn't found any matches for the fingerprints picked up at the break-in, it was likely professionals who know what they're doing."

As I walked out of my office with Hirsch, we were greeted by two uniformed officers—one was Officer Olsen, a familiar face from various crime scenes, and the other was someone I hadn't met. After introductions, I escorted them to the tech center. "Hi, Lewis, this is Sergeant Hirsch and Officers Olsen and Frink. They're here to collect all of Ansel

Griffin's computer artifacts, including any copies of the hard drive."

"Okey-doke, come on in," Lewis said.

The CoCo County team marched in with their boxes and evidence collection materials.

"Have you notified the FBI yet?" I asked.

"I've assigned the case to Jayda. It'll be a top priority in CoCo County, and we'll likely need your help. You've been digging into the background of this guy, I think we're going to have to work together on it," he said, hinting at a smile.

"If we have to," I said, suppressing a grin.

My team had uncovered a network of criminals involved in buying and selling child sex abuse images with financial trails that led to several offshore bank accounts and records over the dark web. A lot of names were listed, roster transactions; all the accounting for the syndicate was on that computer. There was no doubt they would come looking for it, and now that the police were here to collect and process the evidence, it felt reassuring to know armed officers would be escorting it to CoCo County.

"How soon is Jayda going to get started on it?"

"She's in court today, but she told me to schedule a meeting with you for tomorrow morning. She said it would give her some time to go through the notes from your team first."

We had printed out every record and just a few samples of the images—no one needed to see all of them at that moment—and compiled them into a report for CoCo County. It needed to be analyzed further, but my firm decided it was best to let law enforcement do the honors. Because we didn't have the authority to bring the individuals involved to justice or to identify the children in the images and find them, to ensure they were safe. It would be a huge undertaking.

"Looks like it's a typical Martina case: seems small, but quickly turns into a huge case," Hirsch remarked.

"It was Vincent's first."

"But I'm sure you took the lead pretty quick."

"Guilty."

"Hopefully, we can wrap it up pretty soon or hand it off to the feds. They'll have more resources. You've got a big date in a couple of days, don't you?"

"I do, but honestly, I'm not sure we'll have it wrapped up by then. But I can take an evening off every once in a while."

"I'll hold you to that. You're not skipping out on that for anything, OK?" Hirsch's tone was both serious and supportive.

I hadn't planned on it. "As you wish."

Knowing that I'd be working alongside my best friend and Jayda, who was an exceptional detective, assured me that the investigation was in capable hands, and taking a night off to celebrate Charlie's one-year sobriety wouldn't be an issue.

33

MARTINA

From down the hallway, the sounds of Zoey and Kay chattering away reached my ears. I was certain Zoey would welcome Kay's stay with us; Zoey was one of the kindest people I knew. My completely unbiased opinion. It warmed my heart, not only to have my daughter home, but to know that Kay was safe. Becky had chosen to stay with her parents instead, who lived just a few towns over.

As I walked down the hall, Barney greeted me with his usual enthusiasm. Together, we made our way to the kitchen where Zoey and Kay were immersed in an animated conversation.

"Good morning."

"Morning, Mom," Zoey said, her eyes sparkling.

"Good morning, Martina," Kay said, her voice carrying a hint of gratitude.

"How did you sleep, Kay?"

"OK. The bed's really comfortable, and Barney's a nice companion," she said with a small smile forming on her lips. Barney had quickly become her guardian of sorts, wanting to share the bed with her. Barney in a human's bed was an exception I had happily made, to make Kay comfortable. It was a period in Kay's life that was likely more chaotic than most would ever endure. My heart went out to her and her parents, silently hoping for some news from the Ashland PD and NamUs folks about her true identity.

"Yes, Barney's a great little companion."

Zoey said, "Usually, he stays with my grandma and her husband during the day, but since I've been home from school, he gets to stay with us all day." Barney, seemingly understanding he was the topic of discussion, circled around with a wagging tail, visibly happy to be the center of attention.

"Heading off to work this morning?" I asked, shifting the conversation slightly.

Kay said, "Yes. It makes me feel more normal to go into the office."

"Having a routine can definitely help during trying times."

Zoey said, "I told her if she wants to come over tonight, we could have a movie night or a dance party. I learned that Kay also loves Taylor Swift, and she just came out with a new album, and I am super stoked."

Zoey's enthusiasm was infectious. And her love for pop music and her budding friendship with Kay warmed my heart. Kay could use all the comfort and friendship we could offer.

"You're heading off too, Mom?" Zoey asked.

"Yep, heading over to CoCo County actually."

"Working with Uncle August?"

"I am."

Zoey turned to Kay and explained how Hirsch was the sergeant and my bestie that I worked with off and on over the years.

"Who else is going to be there?" Zoey asked.

Zoey had always taken an interest in my work, often attending barbecues and get-togethers with the Cold Case

Squad and the Drakos Monroe team. Her presence was like a burst of sunshine, and it was hard not to love her—a sentiment shared by all, and not just me. She was sparkly, cheerful, and truly the embodiment of sunshine.

"Vincent is coming with me, and Jayda is leading the investigation. We'll likely have to pull in the FBI," I shared, noting Kay's grimace at the mention of the FBI. The complexity of her situation was not lost on any of us, and as we navigated through the day, our collective effort was to provide her with a semblance of normalcy and warmth in our home.

Kay was grappling with a harrowing realization that the man she believed to be her father was, in fact, a pedophile who not only produced but distributed appalling images. The case would gain momentum now that it was in the hands of CoCo County. With the help of their team, I was sure our next step was to revisit the Griffin residence for another search, this time with a focus on uncovering clues related to the criminal enterprise that Ansel seemed deeply entrenched in, possibly even leading.

The complexity of the case was daunting, with numerous transactions and records to sift through, yet no real names were used—only online usernames and special codes. Our upcoming meeting with CoCo County was a procedural step to ensure thorough preparation before involving the FBI. Given the likelihood of the enterprise extending beyond California, possibly even globally, it was imperative to call in federal support as soon as possible.

"I can't believe I never knew," Kay whispered.

"There's no way you could have," I reassured her. "This isn't your fault. It's all on him, not you. There was no way for you to know."

She shrugged, a complex mix of emotions flickering across her face. "Is it weird that I still love him?"

Zoey, sensing the depth of our conversation, quietly picked up Barney.

"Not at all. You thought he was your father. He raised you. But remember, some actions, like locking you in a closet, are indefensible, a form of child abuse," I explained gently. "It's natural to feel sadness for the loss of who you believed he was. You thought he was your only family."

Kay grimaced. "It's true. For so long, I thought he was my whole family, but now I know that's not true. I worry that if or when I reconnect with my biological family, I'm not going to remember them and they'll feel like strangers."

I wished Kay had been open to speaking with a counselor, or someone skilled in navigating such delicate situations. As Zoey handed us coffees, I reassured Kay. "There's an entire team ready to support you, to work with your biological family to prepare them for the possibility that you don't remember them. It will be a challenging adjustment, but how you proceed is entirely your choice. You can meet them and decide from there how you wish to interact with them in the future."

I retrieved a business card from my backpack and offered it to Kay. "Call her. She can guide you through what to expect. It's normal to feel anxious about the future, especially when your entire world has been upended. Remember, no one expects anything from you except to be yourself and do what feels right for you."

She nodded slowly, her eyes reflecting a mix of emotions. "Thank you, for everything. All of this has been so wild. I can barely process any of it."

"That is absolutely understandable," I assured her.

Zoey chimed in. "If you need anything from me, I'm here. I've got movies we can watch and friends if you want to go out— I've got tons of friends home from school. And you'll be safe with me. I've been taking self-defense classes since I was little, right, Mom?"

I couldn't help but smile at her initiative. "I may have been an overprotective mother, but yes, Zoey can take care of herself better than most. And you absolutely could learn too. It's never a bad idea to know how to defend yourself."

Zoey's enthusiasm didn't wane. "We could teach you! Mom even taught a class at Holy Names College with my best friend's older sister. Mom likes to protect people but also to help people protect themselves."

Kay said, "I'm starting to see that."

It was clear to me that Kay needed more than just a distraction; she needed someone to talk to, to help her process the overwhelming revelations about her life.

"I need to head to work, but if you want to call in sick, you're welcome to stay at the house today."

Zoey was quick to help. "Yes! We can plan a whole fun day. Do you like crafts?"

Kay gave her a puzzled look. "Crafts?"

She explained, "I know I might be too old for crafts, glitter, and paint, but it's really calming, especially when I'm anxious about something."

What had Zoey been anxious about? Did I need to worry?

Kay said, "That sounds like fun, maybe after I get home from work. I don't think I've done crafts since elementary school," Kay admitted, a faint smile breaking through.

I had to guess that Kay's upbringing hadn't left much room for such creative outlets. "Okay, if you're ready to go, I'm leaving. You've got my cell phone number, so call me if you need anything. And if you decide you want to come back here, Zoey will be here all day. She's planning to hang out with Barney, and her friend Kaylie might come over too."

"You'd love Kaylie! She's been my best friend for as long as I can remember. She's really fun."

I smiled at my daughter, nearly grown up but still the same old Zoey, always looking to brighten everyone's day in the best way she could. Grabbing a granola bar on my way out, I braced myself for the day ahead, determined to map out the monstrous deeds the man masquerading as Kay's father had committed over the years.

34

MARTINA

AN HOUR LATER, Jayda stood near the whiteboard, her expression serious as she addressed the room. "Boy, it didn't take long to get you guys back in here."

"Can't get rid of us. Like, ever," Vincent replied, with a laugh that edged on malevolent.

I smiled and said, "I told you."

"And I believed you," Jayda said, her smile softening the mood. "OK, so I looked through some of the notes, and yeah, you guys stumbled onto something really serious. So, I know we decided we're going to go through everything here and then put a call into the FBI, but when I started sifting through the notes last night, and then this morning... This thing is massive. So, I put in a call to my friend in the FBI cybercrime task force and sent them the summary you provided. Hopefully they'll be calling soon to let us know if these people are on their radar already or if this is a brand-new, very well-hidden criminal enterprise." Her tone was grave as she continued, "I'm guessing, based on what you've told me about this man, Sidney Thomas, a.k.a. Rex Michels, a.k.a. Ansel Griffin, this is not his first rodeo, and that he's been involved in criminal activity for a long time."

That was what I had been thinking as well. "Exactly. We just don't know how long he's been profiting from it. This guy likely started back before computers were a household item."

Vincent said, "Don't be so sure. Some of the wealthy had computers in their houses in the mid to late '8os. He was a doctor; he probably made good money. After he gave up medicine, he had been profiting from his criminal enterprise which would support the kind of lifestyle of early home computers."

It was a valid point. "Has the team hit the Griffin house yet?" I asked. Kay, Becky, and I had searched the Griffin house but came up empty. But we didn't dig as deep as we could have —like knocking down walls and pulling up carpet.

"We decided to wait to hear from the FBI before going in. They'll want to come in, and I'd like to at least get their advice, so we don't mess anything up."

Hirsch said, "Martina, you took a look at the house with Kay, right?"

"Yeah, but I wasn't looking for anything related to CSAM. We were looking for records of his life before he was Ansel Griffin. He didn't leave much of a paper trail but left quite the electronic one." I added, "But Kay did say that he stashed money in a floorboard, which makes me think if he stashed money in a floorboard, he had other hiding places. We didn't find any at first glance, but if you start knocking down walls, you might find something."

Jayda said, "And if we get the green light from the feds to take a sledgehammer to it, we'll do it." And then she pulled out her cell phone, staring intently at the screen. "That's my guy now."

Her tone shifted as she answered the call. After a brief exchange, she ended the call, and the Polycom on the table rang.

The room held its breath.

Had the FBI known about this guy, or had we really uncovered one of the world's largest threats against children?

35

MARTINA

JAYDA ANSWERED the call on the Polycom. "It's Jayda. I'm here with CoCo County's Sergeant Hirsch and a couple of consultant-friends-discoverers of the hard drive, Martina Monroe and Vincent Teller. You may have heard their names a time or two."

A chuckle resonated from the end of the line. "Oh yeah, we know Martina and Vincent. It's Agent Hammer here from Organized Crime."

"Hello again," I said.

"I see, despite not being with CoCo County, you're still stepping right into the biggest mess you could find, huh?" Hammer's voice held amusement.

"It's a gift, sir," I replied with a smile.

"On the line with me, I've got Special Agent Founders with the CSAM Cyber Crimes Task Force."

I said, "Nice to meet you, Agent Founders."

"Nice to meet you," Vincent added, his voice joining the conversation.

"So, what did you find?" Jayda asked.

"Well, we took a look at the usernames you sent over. And, we have definitely heard of them. We've seen the names as part of an ongoing operation. We had believed they were part of a big organization. And, you said the laptop has financial transactions on it?" Hammer asked.

Jayda said, "It's got transactions, it's got usernames, it's got pictures, and it's got banking records in the Cayman Islands."

"I'd say that's just about the find of the century. Now, we just have to put real identities to those screen names. What happened to the person who owned it?" Hammer's tone shifted slightly.

"Died of a heart attack, according to the Medical Examiner," Jayda informed.

"Well, if the organization knows he's dead, it's possible they're coming for that computer. They'll want to protect it by any means possible," Hammer said with a serious tone.

I said, "I figured as much. A young woman, Kay, was in possession of it because she thought she was Ansel's daughter, but she's not. We now believe Kay was kidnapped when she was four years old. I have her in protective custody in case they come after her."

Hirsch added, "She's staying at Martina's house so nobody will be able to get to her."

"You really do go above and beyond, Martina," Hammer said.

"Well, she has no family that she knows of. I couldn't just let her stay at her apartment. There was already a strange person who came to Ansel's house, pretending to be a coworker, and he wasn't."

"Probably one of the members of the organization. Maybe they heard of his death," Jayda said.

"According to Kay, the man claimed to be named Joe and didn't know Ansel died until she told him. If they didn't know he was dead before, they do now."

"Good to know. We've got a whole team on this, and this

organization. This hard drive, is going to really help us out," Hammer assured.

"Glad to hear it," Jayda said.

It was a relief.

"We don't think they have any idea we're onto them. So, we need to keep this very, very quiet. Not only for the sake of the operation, but to keep Kay safe," Agent Founders added.

"Oh, another thing," Hirsch interjected. "The same guy, Joe, who came by the house went and visited this guy's uncle, who's in a care facility in Pleasant Hill."

"Did the girl know the uncle?" Jayda asked.

I said, "Not until four days ago. She went to talk to him without telling us first."

"Desperate for answers." Jayda sighed. "So, if this uncle is part of the organization, he may have alerted the rest of them that the daughter exists."

I said, "That's what I'm worried about too."

"All right, if you can send us over all the details on the person you were investigating to begin with—who may have been at the top, or at least the accountant or something of that nature—as well as this uncle and the description of the man who visited the house, we'll go and take a look at the house and the care facility," Agent Founders proposed.

Hirsch added, "We did a sweep of the house after it was broken into."

"And the house was broken into? Oh, someone's definitely looking for that computer," Agent Founders said.

Clearly, Jayda hadn't briefed her FBI pals on everything.

"Yes," Hirsch confirmed.

"The FBI will take over from here. We'll be in touch to get all the information and the hard drive. We're not sitting on this; these dudes are bad, and we're gonna take them down," Agent Founders assured.

After coordinating additional details, the call ended, and we all sat quietly, each of us lost in our thoughts.

Breaking the silence, Hirsch said, "Well, Martina, looks like you and Vincent may be partially responsible for bringing down a large criminal organization." He paused. "Again."

Vincent leaned back, hands behind his head, and quipped, "Ah, just another day's work. It's what we do. Take down large criminal organizations."

The room laughed and shook their heads in response.

Hirsch said, "We miss you around here, Vincent."

"What about me?" I interjected.

"And of course, you, Martina," Hirsch said with a wink, bringing a light moment to the tense atmosphere.

Part of me was glad that the FBI was taking over the case, and it was out of our hands because it was dangerous. But that didn't mean Kay was safe. I would keep an eye on her until we got the all-clear. Who knows how long it would take for the FBI to take down these people who had broken into the house and could be coming after that computer. They wouldn't get it, but that didn't mean they knew that. Kay was the most logical person to have possession of the computer, and that made her a target. Until I was sure she was safe, she could stay at my house.

With the criminal investigation off my plate, it was time to finish the job Kay hired us to do—find the little girl Kay referred to as "Sissy," and hopefully identify Kay and find her biological family.

Processing what Mom and Dad told me about my biological father and why we left him was awful. I guess I always assumed it was something like that. Why else would Mom change her name, change mine, and even Grandma and Grandpa too? It was like they were on the run. And Dad, being a US Marshal, knew how to create new identities. Although we weren't technically part of the witness protection program, he had friends in, well, high and low places. They could get the documentation to keep us out of the grasp of my biological father.

Both Mom and Dad swore up and down they didn't know about this little girl I thought was my sister all these years. They told me everything else; I wouldn't think they would lie about that. Maybe I would never know who she was, or why I had created her in my mind. I was a high-functioning person who didn't struggle with depression or anxiety and had loving parents. Maybe the part that wasn't loving, I had blocked out. Maybe I had imagined this other girl, my sister, to help me through those times when I knew about the bad things that had happened to me. A coping mechanism—it's not unheard of and actually can be quite common.

Part of me still felt like she was real, but I knew it was most likely she wasn't. Mom said that my father was capable of the most atrocious things, so who was to say that the girl never existed? Mom theorized that it was possible the girl could have been a neighbor or a daughter of one of his friends. One of his creepy, icky friends—*the monsters*.

After learning about my early years and why we left, I agreed not to pursue private investigators or to look for the girl anymore. She'd be a grown-up now and likely impossible to find. Mom and Dad said they would prefer that I focus on getting counseling to process everything I learned about my early years that I had blocked out. Now it was coming back to me, and that was the strangest part—it was coming back. And those memories with the girl were still there.

Worried about my mental health and ability to process it all, I made my first appointment to speak with a professional. Someone to help me cope with my childhood. Soon enough, I would learn that the girl was all in my imagination, not real at all. And maybe that's why it felt like she was part of me—because she was in *my* imagination.

MARTINA

CLAPPING MY HANDS, I gazed at him as he smiled wide. Everyone cheered for Charlie, who was officially one year sober. The first year is a challenging milestone to reach; the temptation is still fresh, and you're building your support team. I understood it all too well and was grateful for the many years of sobriety I had achieved, having such a strong support team myself, and thankfully, the cravings were never as bad as they used to be. I was proud of Charlie and excited to go out and celebrate.

The fanfare died down, and Charlie said, "Thank you. I don't think I could've made it to this milestone without all of you, but one in particular: Martina."

The room full of AA members applauded me, knowing that we were good friends and had spent a lot of time with each other. Even though Charlie had found his own sponsor—he hadn't asked me, and I hadn't offered—I didn't want that kind of relationship with him. I wanted a friendship and now, perhaps, more.

As he thanked the rest of the group, the moderator ended the session, and we all headed toward the table that held celebratory cupcakes I had brought. Mom had baked them. She said that we couldn't just eat any cake when she had plenty of time on her hands to make him only the best—his favorite, carrot cake with pineapple filling and cream cheese frosting.

Over the past year, Charlie had spent Thanksgiving with us, Christmas, New Year's. He'd become a good family friend. Despite this, he had asked for them not to be there to celebrate. I thought it was a little strange, but I knew he still wrestled with feelings toward his own family and not being able to get a hold of his daughter. He said he'd rather have a small celebration with just me.

Even so, Mom was quite taken with him, as were Hirsch and Zoey. Zoey didn't know him well since she's been away at school, but I had definitely gotten the thumbs-up from her, Mom, and Hirsch. We had never spoken about what would happen once he had his one-year sobriety and he was ready to date someone, and I hadn't brought it up. I was very forward with most of my endeavors, but this was sensitive, and I didn't want to put pressure on Charlie.

As our group leader handed out the treats, Charlie picked up one and handed it to me. The two of us stood next to each other, eating our delicious cake, savoring each morsel, but never taking our eyes off the other.

"Mom said she knew you didn't want to make a fuss, but she couldn't help but be here in her own way," I said with a smile.

"I appreciate it," he said.

We finished our cupcake as many people stopped by and congratulated Charlie and wished him well.

With the crowd thinning and cake finished, I said, "Are you ready for dinner?"

"Almost," he said, a twinkle in his eye. He hurried over to the utility room and returned with a bouquet of flowers—roses. *Red* roses. My heart skipped a beat.

Without a word, he took my hand in his, and we walked outside. It was still light out, and he led me over to a beautiful tree. "And red is for love," he said, words that made my eyes well up with emotion.

Charlie feels it too.

He handed me the flowers, and I said, "I love them."

Charlie looked into my eyes and said, "And I love you. I think I loved you since the first day I met you, Martina. There's always been something about you I couldn't shake. I've been waiting until now to tell you. But I do. I love you. I am head over heels, madly, crazy in love with you, Martina."

Tears welled as I felt like a fool for falling so deeply in love with a man I hadn't been on a single date with. "I love you too, and I haven't been able to shake you either," I said.

He wrapped his arms around me, and we hugged, sniffling and wiping away happy tears. "How about dinner?" he asked.

I nodded.

The restaurant was his pick. I had never been there before, but with the warm summer air, we sat outside at a romantic table. There were twinkly lights on the trellis and candles on the table. It was the most romantic dinner I'd ever been to, no judgment to Jared. He was a wonderful man and a wonderful husband, but he wasn't romantic like this. I felt guilty for a moment, thinking about Jared. He'd been gone for so long, and I started to wonder how he'd feel about me falling in love again. But I knew Jared, and I'd like to think he would want me to be happy. Part of me couldn't believe any of this was real—that I had found the second love of my life, and he loved me too.

As we sat across from one another, conversation was easy—it always had been—but now there was something else. There were plans for the future, and I almost couldn't respond when he asked me officially if it was all right if he referred to me as his girlfriend. Even though we were both in our 40s, it seemed an odd term, but he couldn't think of anything else. I laughed and said, "It is a bit strange to be called a girlfriend in my 40s, but yes, I'll be your girlfriend."

"Thank the lord!"

We both smiled, and after the server took our plates away, he placed his hands on the table, and I placed mine atop his. He held my hands in his, leaned forward, and I sat up.

Over the candlelight, we shared our first kiss.

It was short and sweet, but it was a moment I knew I would never forget. We sat back down, trying to behave ourselves. I guessed he had been waiting for the moment for as long as I had. When the waiter returned and asked if we wanted dessert, we both promptly replied "No." Not because we were avoiding sugar but because we craved being alone together, *finally*.

As we walked out of the restaurant hand-in-hand, my cell phone vibrated in my pocket. "I should get that, in case it's Zoey."

He nodded.

Sure enough, I answered, "Hey, Zoey, what's going on?"

"Mom, there's someone on the cameras."

In an instant, I snapped out of my romantic bliss and said, "What do you mean there's someone on the cameras?"

"In the back yard. I can see it on the monitor; there's someone here."

"Call the police right away. Call Uncle August. Let them know immediately; they'll send someone in an instant. I'm on my way."

"OK, thanks, Mom." Realizing I was leaving my daughter to defend herself, I asked, "Is Kay there?"

"She is."

"Have Kay call the police and then Hirsch. I'll stay on the phone with you."

I looked at Charlie, and he quickly said, "I'll drive; you stay on the phone."

Charlie and I hurried to his car.

My thoughts began to swirl: Who was the man, and was he there for Kay? Would he hurt her? Would he hurt Zoey? The fear for their safety overshadowed the warmth of the evening, turning a night of celebration into one filled with fear.

38

MARTINA

When we arrived at my house, three police cars and Hirsch were surrounding the front of our home. I had been on the phone with Zoey the entire time, but thankfully, the CoCo County Sheriff's Department had someone in the area and was able to respond within minutes to the house. Zoey and Kay were safe.

We parked, and I hurried up the driveway, not waiting for Charlie. I knew he'd understand. I was greeted by a police officer who stood outside the front door.

"Hi, I'm Martina Monroe. I live here, and Charlie is behind me," I said, as Charlie hurried up. "He's with me." And despite the high emotions of the moment, I paused when I realized he was with me—we were together. Shaking the thoughts from my mind, I focused on the officer.

"I'm going to need some identification, ma'am."

Hirsch spotted us in the hallway. "Officer, it's fine. That's Martina and Charlie." He hesitated slightly, gave me a look, and I couldn't help but suppress a smile. Despite the seriousness, he waved me over.

"Hey, Hirsch," I greeted him with a hug. "Thanks for getting here so soon."

"Of course."

"Where are Zoey and Kay?"

"They're inside. Jayda and another officer are interviewing them," he said, "Hi Charlie, good to see you."

"You too. Wish it wasn't under such circumstances," Charlie replied.

Hirsch nodded, and then I heard Zoey coming down the hall. "Mom!"

I hugged my not-so-little girl and asked, "Are you okay?"

"I don't know if I've ever been so scared, Mom."

It nearly broke my heart. "I know, but you see how quick they got here. I'll always protect you, and so will Uncle August."

Hirsch said, "That's for sure."

"I feel so bad for Kay. She's a wreck, Mom."

I could only imagine what that poor woman was going through. "I'm glad you're safe. What made you think to check the monitors?"

"Barney started barking, and so then I checked the monitors, and sure enough, a man was in the back yard."

Thankfully, we had surveillance cameras, and whoever it was, his image would be captured on film. And of course, I didn't skimp and save on my security system; it was state-of-the-art, the best there was on the market. We had whoever this guy was.

We headed toward the living room where Kay sat with Jayda and a uniformed officer. Jayda waved. "Hey, Martina."

"Hi, Jayda," I said. "Thanks for coming out."

She headed toward me. "I was just talking to Kay. I came out when I heard the call. I assumed, based on our conversation yesterday, that it could be linked to our case. And we think it is.

Kay says the guy on the camera is the same guy who came to the Griffin house and visited the uncle."

"Do you have any idea who he is?" I asked.

She shook her head. "No, but I'll contact Agent Founders at the cyber crime task force. We'll run them through facial recognition. We'll figure out who this guy is and make sure he can't come anywhere near her again. Or your house."

"Thanks." I hesitated when I eyed Charlie and then said, "Jayda, this is Charlie. I don't think you've met."

Jayda gave Charlie a look and then said, "It's very nice to meet you, Charlie. I've heard a lot about you."

"Likewise," Charlie said.

I looked over Jayda's shoulder and caught a glance at Kay. She was in tears, holding tissues tightly in her grip.

To the small group, including Zoey and Charlie, I said, "I want to talk to her," and made my way over to Kay, who was sitting on my sofa. A uniformed officer was next to her, taking diligent notes as Kay spoke.

She paused and said, "Hi, Martina."

"How are you doing?" I asked gently.

"Bad," she admitted.

"Well, I'm glad you were here and not at your apartment."

"I don't think I've ever been more scared. And then the police were here, and I'm telling you, after I called, it only took like two minutes to get here."

"The sheriff's department knows my phone number. They take care of us here."

"It was him, Martina. You're right; he's after me. What am I gonna do?"

Kay was understandably frightened. "You're going to stay with me, and you're going to be safe."

"But surely I can't stay here forever?"

"Have faith. Jayda, she's heading up the investigation for

CoCo County and is working with the FBI. She's one of the very best. I've worked with her and known her for many years, and Sergeant Hirsch is top-notch. They won't rest until they catch this guy. Okay?"

"He's the one Zoey told me about. Uncle August?"

"Yep."

"Okay."

"Don't worry. This will all get settled. Have you made a call to the counselor yet?"

She shook her head. "I will."

"Okay."

She looked over and saw Charlie. "I'm so sorry. You had your big date tonight."

"It's okay. Your safety is more important," I reassured.

"I'm so sorry I put Zoey and you at risk. I feel terrible."

"Nonsense, you came to me for help. This is how I help. Nobody's getting to you or Zoey or me."

She nodded.

"I do think it's best that you stay in the house for a while, or we can move you to another safe house. But the police will make sure this guy doesn't come anywhere near this house again."

Hirsch was behind me, and I glanced up at him. He said, "That's right. In addition to the security system, we will have police stationed outside the house until the case has been resolved and this guy has been caught. Okay?"

"Thank you, Sergeant Hirsch."

"Anytime."

Next on the list of things to do was catch this guy and ensure Kay and my family were safe. Despite my optimism, I worried about Zoey's safety and Kay's. A patrol car was good, the security system was good, but I didn't like that someone was on my property, threatening my family and my client.

39

KAY

IT TOOK Martina and her team, along with the police, less than 24 hours to find the man who said his name was Joe. They arrested him based on the surveillance footage and the statements I had given to the police. I had no idea when I walked into that private investigator's office trying to find my mother and my sister's graves that I would learn not only that Dad was not my dad but that I had, mostly likely, been kidnapped by a predator when I was four years old.

We still hadn't heard back from the NamUs people to let me know if I was that girl, Kaitlyn Ramsey. I couldn't let myself believe it was true yet. I would wait until the official news, even though I saw the photo—she looked just like me. And it made sense that my name would be Kaitlyn. I always remembered being referred to as Kay and never had a memory of having a different name.

Martina said I could stay with her as long as I wanted—until I felt safe, but I felt bad about putting her and her daughter in danger. I didn't think I'd ever met anybody quite like Martina.

I grew up without a mother, and watching Zoey and

Martina together was like witnessing the kind of relationship you only saw on TV or dreamed of if you didn't have a mom yourself. She was warm, strong, and protective. I had strong and protective growing up, from Ansel, but I didn't have warm. I didn't have someone's shoulder to cry on. Ansel, or whatever his name was, didn't like tears. If I cried, I would be locked in the closet. So, I learned not to cry. Part of me felt relieved that he wasn't my dad, but the other part felt lost and confused. Why did I still miss him? Love him? I was really conflicted about that, but knowing all the things he had likely done to me, what a bad man he really was, I was still glad I wasn't his daughter.

But I didn't want to stay with Martina anymore—I mean, I did, but she had already done so much for me. I was about to write a note letting her know that I was leaving and going back to my apartment when she walked into the kitchen and said, "Hey, Kay, what's going on?"

"Oh, I was just thinking about going back to my apartment. You know, since they caught the guy who had been following me."

Martina's forehead wrinkled up like she was concerned. "You're welcome to stay here. I don't think it's safe yet."

"Do you think it's safe for me to go to work?"

Martina was quiet for far too long, like she was contemplating whether I could even go to work. "Maybe I can drive you there and pick you up. That way, nobody can follow you."

Her offer was yet another testament to her kindness and the protective nature she held over those she cared for. In that moment, I realized the depth of her generosity and the safe haven she offered, not just a place to stay.

Now she was willing to be my chauffeur.

How were there people like Martina in the world but also people like Ansel and that man supposedly named Joe? His name was Jacob Hauser, apparently, and he didn't have a criminal record at all, which was weird. But neither had my father—I mean, Ansel. He didn't have a criminal record either, but he was a terrible person.

"OK, I'll let you drive me." It sounded like a weird thing to say—let her drive me. I just needed to not be sitting in the house all day. Even though I was scared now that they had come after me, like Martina had cautioned. But I needed something normal, something familiar. Work was the only place I could go that could make me feel that way.

Martina, with a reassuring smile, said, "OK, then it's settled. Make sure you call that counselor too."

"I already left a message."

"Perfect."

"Is there anything I can do to help out around here? I mean, you've been so gracious. Can I clean the bathrooms or something?"

Martina cocked her head and said, "Nonsense, you're a guest. Speaking of, Zoey and I were talking about ordering dinner. We were thinking, maybe since you're here with us, we could do another movie night. Something relaxing—order pizza, and stay in."

"I'd really like that."

Martina's smile was comforting. "Okay, then. All I'll need is your list of favorite pizza toppings."

After I explained that I loved a good pepperoni pizza, she smiled and said, "Zoey will be thrilled."

"If I didn't already say it before, Martina, thank you—thank you for everything. You saved my life and kind of gave me one too."

She patted me on the shoulder and said, "You're very welcome."

Martina's actions spoke volumes about the kind of person she was—selfless, caring, and protective. In a world where darkness seemed to lurk at every corner, she was a beacon of light, offering not just shelter but a sense of belonging and family to someone who had been searching for it their entire life.

40

MARTINA

Staring at the beautiful bouquet of multi-colored roses, I thought I could probably get used to the romantic gifts. Another gift from Charlie—the first one a cryptic message: yellow roses for friendship. Then red roses on our first date and a declaration of love. It was unlike anything I've ever felt before. Who knew that I would've found someone at a rehabilitation center? Hirsch told me over lunch that he had anticipated I would've met a lawyer, a judge, or a marshal—someone tough and on the right side of the law, a left-brained person, not a creative, romantic type like Charlie. But he agreed, Charlie was perfect for me. And I tended to agree.

It was like how Kim complemented Hirsch as the bubbly, playful, beautiful, intelligent teacher she was—soft, warm, and kind—she had softened Hirsch along with Audrey, their daughter. But she was his perfect match too, and now I had found mine. The yin to my yang, the creative to my justice-driven, tough career.

I pulled out the card and read it.

Dear Martina,
Yellow for friendship, Red for love. I'm grateful
that I have both of those with you. Can't wait to
see you.
Love, Charlie.

IT WAS TRUE, the experts always say it's best to be friends first to have a solid foundation for a relationship. We had spent an entire year getting to know each other, to enjoy each other's company without complicating it with physical things.

He'd been so understanding about cutting the end of our date short to rush to the house. He stayed until all the police were gone and he knew that we were settled in okay. He stayed for a late-night snack, and I walked him to the car. I got another kiss, this time more passionate, and I couldn't wait for what was coming next.

"Look at you. You're gonna be the envy of everybody in this office," Vincent said.

"I suppose I'm okay with that."

"I'm guessing your date with Charlie went well?"

"It did, but of course, it was interrupted."

"I heard. How is Kay holding up?"

"I dropped her off at work this morning. She said she needed to be somewhere familiar, somewhere that she knew. I think it'll help calm her."

"And has Hirsch questioned Jacob Hauser?" Vincent asked.

"He says they're doing everything they can to get this guy to talk, but he's not saying a word."

"At least Kay's safe with you, and you had the foresight to know that she needed protection."

"I'm not totally convinced she's in the clear yet. The fact Hauser went to my house to get to Kay and the laptop is telling about how far the organization will go to get it. I'm guessing with him in custody, they'll lay low for a little bit. That'll give the police and the FBI some time to track down the identity of all these people. Having Hauser in custody should help them do that."

"Fingers crossed."

"Indeed."

"Anyhow, there's an update."

"Update with what?"

"Just got a call from the detective in Ashland, Oregon who had been in charge of the Kaitlyn Ramsey kidnapping." He paused. "The DNA is a match for Kay and Kaitlyn Ramsey. Kaitlyn Ramsey has been found."

It was just like Vincent to not lead with the most exciting news. Although it was what we had suspected. "That's great. Not entirely surprising since the face was a match, the name, where she'd gone missing from, and where we knew Ansel Griffin had been during those years," I said. "Have the parents been notified?"

"Yes, and the Ashland Police Department asked us to have a call with them. They have questions, obviously. The parents asked to speak with us since we've been working with Kay."

"All right. Did they say when they wanted to have a call?"

Vincent smiled, that knowing look like he'd already made the appointment. "Now."

I had to admit, Vincent kept me on my toes. "Now it is."

We headed down the hallway into one of the conference rooms that had a projector. Up on the screen was what looked like a police detective and a man and a woman in tears huddled next to each other. I recognized them from the social media photos. It was Kaitlyn's parents. I waved as I walked in and sat down next to Vincent. "Hello, I'm Martina Monroe."

"Hi, I am Detective Prime from Ashland PD, and this here is Mr. and Mrs. Ramsey."

"Hello, it's very nice to meet you."

"Detective Prime said that you found our daughter. You found Kaitlyn?"

I nodded. "Yes, we did."

"How did you know she was our Kaitlyn?"

Vincent and I exchanged glances, and I said, "It's a bit of a long story, but..." I explained everything from the first time she walked into our offices, that she'd been looking for her family's graves, to the DNA test proving she wasn't Ansel Griffin's daughter and the fact that Kay was currently at her job where she worked as a communication manager for a law firm, and while we were finding her family, she was staying with mine. I left out the huge criminal organization we'd uncovered or that we suspected Kay had been abused. That was for another time.

"So, she's healthy, though? Can you tell us about her?" Kaitlyn's mother asked, her voice laced with years of worry and hope.

"Kay is a lovely young woman, caring and smart. She has some good friends who have been helping her through this. Also, I've given her the name of a counselor to help her process everything she has learned over the past few weeks. She's going through a lot, and she did share with me that she has some anxiety about finding her biological family. She doesn't remember being taken. She doesn't remember a family before Ansel Griffin. The only thing she remembers from her childhood, other than Ansel, was a little girl she called 'Sissy.' Do you have another daughter?"

"No. A son." Mrs. Ramsey shook her head. "Our poor baby girl... I never gave up, though. I knew she was still out there. I knew it... I just knew it." She cried, and even I got a little teared up. Her parents had never given up—21 years their daughter had been missing. It was against all odds to have found her alive.

The Ramseys turned to Detective Prime. "When do we get to see her?"

Detective Prime said, "That's why we wanted to have this conference call with you, Martina and Vincent. Since she's staying at Martina's house and you seem to have gotten to know her, how do you think we should best approach this? The Ramseys would like to fly down to California as soon as possible to see her, but we need to understand if she's ready or if she wants to come up to Oregon. But they're packed and ready."

"Let me speak to Kay. You're welcome to meet her at my house or somewhere neutral. I'll ask her how she's feeling, what she'd like to do."

Her father nodded and said, "We just want what's best for her. We talked to the detective and the family liaison. We know she might not remember us, and that's okay, but we remember her like it was yesterday." His voice cracked, and emotion filled the room.

"I'll call Kay and have a conversation with her. Let her know what we've found. Okay?"

"All right. Can we give you all our information?"

I smiled and said, "Absolutely. I'll talk to Detective Prime, and we'll work out the logistics to make sure everybody's comfortable so that you have the best meeting possible, considering the circumstances."

They nodded.

"Do you have a picture? A recent one?"

I didn't, other than her driver's license photo. "I'm sorry, I don't. But she's a beautiful young woman. She doesn't look that different than she did when she was four. She's a little leaner, but looking at her picture at four and looking at her now, there's not much doubt it's her."

They smiled through tears, and I promised to be in touch with them as soon as I could. After goodbyes and exchange of information, we ended the teleconference.

Vincent said, "Man, and that's why we do this job, huh?"

"Seriously. It makes all the bad stuff worth it."

"I can't imagine having a child stolen from you. Being a parent seems so scary."

"It is." I looked at him. "But it's very rewarding, Vincent."

"I hope so," he said, a smile creeping onto his face.

"Is Amanda..." I asked, without asking.

He nodded with a sparkle in his eyes. "She's 16 weeks along."

"Congratulations, Vincent! Oh, I'm so happy for you and Amanda. You're going to make a wonderful father."

"I hope so. It scares the bejeezus out of me."

"Parenting does that." Delighted with the news and the number of happy tears being shed, I went back to my office to call Kay. I dialed her cell phone, but she didn't answer. Maybe it was because she didn't recognize my desk phone number. Personally, I didn't answer many calls on my cell phone from numbers I didn't know.

Picking up my cell phone, I dialed her number again. As the phone rang and rang, it went to voicemail. Maybe she was busy at work. I looked up the information for her office phone; that went to voicemail too. With a sinking feeling, I grabbed my backpack, about to rush out when I realized I could call the main number. I sat back down and called the law offices of Vine and Plank where she worked.

"Law offices of Vine and Plank, how may I help you?"

"Yes, I'm looking for Kay Griffin. I tried her desk and wasn't able to get her."

"Oh, she's probably around here somewhere. I saw her

earlier; hold on, let me check." It must be a small office for her to get up and search the office.

Maybe I was being overprotective, worrying over nothing. Surely, I was being paranoid. The woman returned to the phone, "I think she's in a meeting. Can I leave a message?"

"Sure, it's Martina. Just have her call me. She has my number."

"Will do."

Vincent appeared in the doorway, "Get a hold of her?"

"No, she's not answering, but I called her work, and they said that she's in a meeting."

I glanced at the clock on the wall. I'd try again in another half hour. Or wait to see her in person. This wasn't a conversation to have over the phone.

"Maybe I should wait until she's done with her workday."

"It is quite the news, Martina. Life-changing news. I don't think she'd want to wait."

He was right. And I couldn't help but think of her parents waiting on pins and needles for us to call with the details, for them to see their daughter after 21 long years. I'd head over as soon as she called me back. It was news she would want to hear.

41

MARTINA

An hour later, I still hadn't heard back from Kay. I assumed she was still in meetings; it was a Monday, and as the communication manager for the law firm, she probably had a lot of work to do, especially since she'd been out of the office after Ansel's death. But when I received a frantic call from her friend Becky, I knew I needed to find her, see her face, and make sure she was okay. I hopped in my car and drove over to Kay's place of work.

Standing in front of the reception desk at the law office, I said, "Hi, I'm Martina, and I'm here to see Kay Griffin."

"Sure, let me go see where she's at. Last time I checked, she was in a meeting. Oh, you called, right?"

"Yes, I'm the one who called. I haven't gotten a call back from her. Has she been in a meeting this whole time?"

"It's been so busy here today. I'm not entirely sure. Let me go check her desk," she said cheerfully and hurried back into the offices.

I glanced around the room. It was a swanky office with strange-looking art on the walls that was probably very expensive, gold letterhead on the walls as well, and the furniture was sleek, mid-century modern contemporary. Hopefully, I didn't alarm Kay by just showing up unannounced. I didn't like that she hadn't returned my call. There could be a very reasonable explanation for why she hadn't, but considering she had texted Becky she would meet her thirty minutes earlier for coffee and didn't show up, the situation didn't feel right to me. It was possible Kay had gotten caught up at work, but I couldn't ignore my instincts. I learned long ago that if I had an instinct, I needed to listen to it. It wasn't always right, but most of the time, it was. I'd rather be safe than sorry—have Kay surprised to see me and letting me know that she was too busy at work to have a conversation than it be something much worse.

After what seemed like several minutes, I glanced at the time on my watch, and sure enough, it had been three minutes. For the size of the office, three minutes wasn't that long, but maybe the receptionist got caught up in a conversation and got sidetracked and hadn't been able to find Kay right away. The young woman who had been behind the reception desk returned with a middle-aged woman wearing a tailored suit.

"Hi, my name is Carol Ann Henson. You're looking for Kay?"

"Yes, I am. Is she available?"

"Is she expecting you?"

"No, but I've called a few times, and she was supposed to meet a friend for coffee and didn't show. She's currently staying with me due to some personal issues. I planned to pick her up at 5 o'clock, which is when she said the workday ended, but there was some news I wanted to share with her. Is she here?"

"I'm not sure where she is. She doesn't have any meetings on her calendar, and I checked in with the partners, and they haven't seen her either. It could be that she went out for a walk or ran some errands and lost track of time."

It was possible. "She didn't have her car. And if she had been on a walk, she would have her phone, right?"

Carol Ann was quiet.

"Do you have security cameras?"

"Building management does. We don't have access to them here. Did you want me to call to see if she's been outside? Are you worried?"

"Yes, I am worried. Please call."

"Okay..." She turned to the receptionist. "Have you checked the ladies' room?"

"No, I hadn't thought of that."

Carol Ann hurried back without another word but quickly returned. "She's not in there either. She's not here."

"Please call the building manager for the surveillance footage."

Carol Ann nodded and pulled out her cell phone.

Turning to the receptionist, I said, "Have you seen Kay today?"

"Yes, this morning, but I don't think I saw her after that. But it's been a really busy day. She could've slipped out."

Carol Ann ended her call. "I've asked them to send over the last hour's footage to see if they can spot her on camera leaving the building. I was in a meeting with Kay about an hour ago, and it's been about forty-five minutes since it ended. That should be sufficient."

At least we had a relatively narrow timeline. "Thank you. Did they say how long it will take to send the footage?"

"Five to ten minutes. They're on site," she said. "Are you worried something happened? She told me that there's been a lot going on, and she's only been back for a few days since her father died."

"Has she shared with you what she's learned over these last few weeks?"

She shook her head. "But she told me she was staying with someone because she could be in danger."

"Yes, she is. And, honestly, I'm very worried."

Carol Ann said, "Hopefully the surveillance footage will give us answers."

"Can you check her desk to see if she left her cell phone there?"

"Of course. I'll be right back."

While Carol Ann went in search of the phone, I called Vincent. "Hey."

"Did you find her?"

My heart sank. "No, I think she's gone." I had just told her parents that she'd been found, and now here she was missing again.

"Like really gone?"

Carol Ann returned, looking frantic and shaking her head, a signal that she hadn't found Kay's phone. I told Vincent to hold on. "No sign of the phone?" I asked Carol Ann.

"I don't see it anywhere."

With a nod, I lifted the phone back up to my ear. "Can we track her cell phone? I know we're not supposed to do that, but I'm worried."

"I'm on it."

"Thanks, I'll call Hirsch."

"I'll let you know what I find."

Ending the call, I quickly dialed Hirsch. "Martina, what's up?"

I explained the events leading up to this moment. He said, "I'll put out an APB on her."

"Thanks, Hirsch. I also, off the record, may have someone who is doing a trace on her cell phone."

"I didn't hear that, but let me know if you find something on the video."

With the end of the phone call, I wondered if we'd find Kay in time. I thought, *When will that surveillance footage get here?*

42

KAY

MY BODY SHOOK, and panic began to take over. I found myself in darkness, disoriented, unsure if it was a closet—perhaps the old closet Ansel used to lock me in. Everything happened in a flash; one moment I was standing outside, the next, my vision blurred, and I was dragged into a van.

When I awoke, my memories were fragmented, only piecing together how I had gotten inside this dark room. The person who took me hadn't spoken to me. But I must have been unconscious for a while.

Why had they taken me? Was it as Martina said—that the people associated with Ansel would come after me for the laptop? It was the only explanation that made sense.

Suddenly, the door opened, and light spilled into the darkness. Squinting, I raised my hand to shield my eyes. A large, strong hand seized my arm, pulling me from what I now realized was indeed a closet, but not the one from my old house.

The tall, burly man wore a ski mask.

In desperation, I cried out, "What do you want? Who are you?" as he dragged me down a dark hall into a room with only a floor lamp, a chair, and a small table. No windows.

"Be quiet," he demanded, his voice a stern whisper.

"I don't have it. I don't have the laptop. I don't have anything," I screamed.

He pushed me down into the hard chair.

"You say you don't have the laptop? How do you know that's what I want?" he asked.

"The laptop... Ansel's laptop. I figured it was what you wanted. I don't have it," I stuttered.

Arms crossed, he said, "Why do you think I want it?"

I recalled the warning to keep silent about the laptop's whereabouts and what might be on it. But if not telling this man cost me my life, was it worth it? Or was my fate sealed either way? "Did you kill Ansel?"

"No," came his blunt reply.

This man couldn't be Joe; that man was behind bars. Who was this guy? Was he one of the creepy guys who preyed on children? How many were there? Would Martina and the police find me in time?

The man said, "I'll ask you one more time, why do you think I want it?"

He really wasn't going to let up. "It's the only thing I had of Ansel's."

Shaking his head, he said, "Where is it?"

"Someone broke into my house and took it. It's gone," I said, hoping he bought the explanation.

"Are you saying someone broke into your apartment?"

My heart beat so fast I could hear it in my ears. "No. The house. Ansel's house. The burglar must have taken it."

He knelt down in front of me and stared with wide brown eyes. "Now I know you're lying."

"I'm not."

"You are. I was the one who broke in. I didn't take it. That means you're lying. I don't care much for liars."

"The police searched the house too. Maybe they took it."

"The police searched the house?"

"Yes. The last I heard, they intended to search behind the walls and under the floorboards. They're turning everything upside down," I said, hoping he'd spare my life if I told him something.

"Why would they go to such lengths for a simple burglary? What have you told them? Did you access the laptop?" he asked, still within inches of my face.

"I didn't, I swear. The police have it," I blurted out, hoping this confession wouldn't seal my fate or ruin the police's case. "Let me go. I don't know anything," I pleaded.

"I don't think we can do that. Stay put," he stated coldly before exiting the room.

He didn't restrain me, likely knowing escape was impossible. A sinking realization hit me; they may have no intention of releasing me. I may die in this sad, empty room.

43

MARTINA

Vincent called while I waited, impatiently, for the building manager to show up with the surveillance footage. He said, "We've got a location on her cell phone, but I'm not sure how useful it's going to be. It's in the vicinity of her office building. So, she's either still there, or if somebody took her, they tossed it."

"Can you pinpoint where we should be looking for it?"

"It's likely in the building or parking lot. When they bring the surveillance video, tell them you need any footage they have of the outside of the building and the entrance and exits to the parking lot. If they don't have the entrance and exits, I'll check the area for traffic cams. If Kay was taken by car, we'll need to know what car she's in."

That was Vincent, always one step ahead.

Just as I was about to end the call with Vincent, the receptionist received a call. She looked at me and nodded solemnly. Placing the phone back down, she announced, "They have it. Said they'll bring it right down and show you on their laptop."

"Perfect, thank you. Did you hear that, Vincent?"

"I did. I have the location of her office building. Do you

want me to call Hirsch and get traffic camera footage from the surrounding streets, or I can do a rush job," Vincent offered.

A rush job meant hack into the system or use other illegal means. "I'll call Hirsch. Do what you need to do."

A few minutes later, a man in a wrinkled suit hurried through the front door. "Hi, I'm Travis Broderick from office management. I have the surveillance footage you asked for," he said to the receptionist. I hurried over, as did the office manager, Carol Ann.

The receptionist said, "This is Martina Monroe, and this is Kay's manager, Carol Ann Henson. They wanted to see the footage."

He then looked up and asked, "You think this girl might've been taken?"

"Nobody's seen her in the last forty-five minutes, and she's connected to a very dangerous set of criminals," I explained.

"Oh my," Travis said. "Well, I'll show you what we have. We save everything on a hard drive. I've put it on a thumb drive so I could show you on my laptop. Is there a conference room we can go into?"

Carol Ann led us back into the office area and into a conference room. Mr. Broderick sat down, opened the lid to his laptop and pulled up the footage.

"What time do you think she was taken?" he asked, his fingers poised over the keyboard.

"Her friend texted Kay to meet her outside at 2:10. Our theory is that she went out before that, just a few minutes earlier, and was taken in that timeframe. So, maybe anywhere from 2 to 2:10?" I speculated, hoping the narrow timeframe would bring back footage of Kay quickly. If it didn't, we would have to widen the time frame.

I waited, a bundle of nerves, for the video footage to start playing.

Travis pointed. "This is the entrance to the office here. As you can see, there are shadows and a bit of a blind spot on the left, around the corner."

Processing the information, I didn't comment, rather my eyes remained glued to the screen, hoping to catch a glimpse of Kay, or more accurately, Kaitlyn Ramsey.

At 2:05, the door opened, and a figure emerged. The video quality wasn't the best, but I could tell it was Kay because of her outfit, which was the same one I had seen her in when I dropped her off that morning, and her unmistakable hair and build. As we watched, I held my breath, fearing the worst.

Sure enough, timestamped 90 seconds later, a figure rushed at her, wrapped his hand around her mouth, and dragged her around the corner. I said, "Rewind that and freeze the image of the kidnapper." The assailant was about a foot taller than Kay— so my guess was 6'3", a male with a rather large build. Wearing a mask, no facial features were distinguishable, and he wore gloves. This didn't bode well for the investigation.

Carol Ann gasped. "Oh my gosh, she was taken."

Closing my eyes briefly, I said, "That's what I suspected. Do you have video of the entrance and exits to the parking lot?"

"No, sorry. We just have cameras pointing at the building."

"Okay. I'm going to step out as I need to make a phone call. Can you please give me a copy of that? I need to forward it to the CoCo County Sheriff's Department." A surge of guilt ripped through me. I should have told Kay not to leave the building for any reason except for me to pick her up.

"Yes, of course. I brought you a copy," Travis replied, lifting a small thumb drive. I thanked him before stepping out and into the hallway to call Vincent.

After he answered, I said, "Vincent, she was taken. It's right on video—2:05 PM this afternoon. The man, around 6'3", large build, ski mask. I need all cameras around there checked."

"I'm on it. Have you called Hirsch yet?"

"I was just about to."

"OK, talk to you later."

Before I could dial, Hirsch called. Absent of pleasantries, he said, "You find anything?"

"Yes," I explained, detailing everything we had seen on the surveillance footage.

"All right, I'll dispatch a team down to the office building to check for that cell phone and see if she's still there. If they grabbed her, maybe they're holding her somewhere on-site."

"Vincent said we should get traffic camera footage from the surrounding areas to get a look at any cars leaving the parking lot around that time. He's working on it."

"I have no comment. I'll have my team work on obtaining the traffic cam footage."

He knew better than to ask for clarification.

My heart pounding, I said, "We need to find her."

"We will," he said. "I'll notify the FBI and Jayda's team that Kay is now officially missing."

I shook my head in disbelief. A little girl kidnapped 21 years ago was found alive, and within 24 hours of us learning her true identity, she was kidnapped again. What kind of cruel fate was that?

44

MARTINA

Standing outside the law office, I waited anxiously for Hirsch and his team to arrive. The search of the building was a necessary step, albeit one I was skeptical would yield results. Kay's phone had been located here, which was a lead, but the chances of her still being in the building felt slim. My focus was on praying we received the traffic cam footage of all vehicles exiting the parking lot around the time of her abduction as soon as possible. We knew we were likely looking for something large enough to transport an unwilling passenger—possibly a van or a truck with a camper shell.

My phone vibrated, slicing through my train of thought. Hoping it was Hirsch, I was instead greeted by an unfamiliar number. The area code, however, was recognizable, and my heart sank with the anticipation of the call. "Martina Monroe," I answered.

"Hi Martina, this is Detective Prime. I'm calling on behalf of Kaitlyn Ramsey's parents. Have you gotten a chance to talk to her?"

In that moment, a heaviness settled on my heart. For reasons

I couldn't fathom, the words wouldn't come—speaking the reality aloud felt too tragic.

"Martina?" His voice brought me back.

"Sorry, I'm just going to say it. The update we gave you... about how we were able to identify Kay and her links to the suspect... I didn't tell you everything. Ansel, her kidnapper, was part of a criminal organization. There's a laptop with a lot of sensitive information on it. Kay has been staying with me, out of fear that someone might think she has the laptop and would come after her."

I could hear the detective's soft, disheartened murmur. "Oh, no."

"I called her earlier to tell her that we had a positive identification and that I've spoken with her parents, but I couldn't get a hold of her. And then I got a call from a good friend of hers. She went to meet Kay at her work, but Kay didn't show up and wasn't answering her calls. I hurried down to her workplace. Long story short, we just reviewed surveillance footage and Kay's been taken. We've got everybody from the CoCo County Sheriff's Department looking for her, plus my team tracking traffic cam footage—we'll find her." I prayed.

"I don't know how I'm going to tell her parents," he confessed, likely the weight of the situation pressing down on him—*hard*.

I shook my head, a silent echo of his sentiment. I wouldn't know how to do it either.

As I remained on the phone with Detective Prime, Hirsch arrived, accompanied by three other black-and-white patrol cars. I waved to him, signaling the urgency of the situation.

As Hirsch approached, I explained to Detective Prime I needed to put him on hold. To Hirsch, I said, "Hey."

"We'll do our search as fast as we can. How is Vincent coming along with the traffic cams?" Hirsch asked.

"I'm still waiting to hear." With each passing moment, Kay's safety hung more precariously in the balance. "I'm on a call with the detective from Ashland, Oregon. Where her biological parents are from."

Hirsch shook his head in disbelief at the situation. "All right. Good luck."

Returning to my conversation with Detective Prime, I said, "Hi. We have a set of officers here to search the office building. It's up to you if you want to tell the parents or not. Like I said, we've got everybody on this. We are going to find Kay," I assured him, though the words felt hollow. We would find her, but would it be in time?

My phone buzzed, signaling another call—this time from Vincent. "Detective Prime, I'm gonna have to call you back. That's Vincent—he may have an update. Maybe hold off on telling the parents; just give us a little time. I'll keep you updated, I promise."

"I'll hold off, but let's keep in touch," he said.

I was sure he didn't want to deliver the news any more than I did. Ending the call with Detective Prime, I immediately switched to Vincent, eager for any shred of progress. "Vincent, what have we got?"

"I think we have three potential vehicles. We've got license plate numbers for all. One is a dark panel van, perfect for a kidnapping scenario. The second is a truck, but we couldn't see inside the bed, so someone could be hidden there under a tarp—unclear, but it's a possibility. The third option is a minivan, easily used to conceal an unwilling passenger."

"OK, run the plates," I instructed, my voice steady despite the turmoil within.

"Are you sure? I mean, I can," he hesitated, the implication of stepping into legal quicksand not lost on him.

Lowering the phone momentarily, I turned to Hirsch, who

had been closely following the exchange. "He's got license plate numbers."

"I'll call it in. Have him send the plate numbers to my cell."

"Vincent, you hear that?"

"Sure did. I'll send them now and start my own investigation."

Of course he would. For all I cared, the legalities could be gone with the wind. Kay's life was far more important.

45

MARTINA

Restless, waiting for the suspect information, I went home to check on Zoey and Barney and, of course, to call Becky to let her know what was going on and to advise her to stay away from the apartment. Upon entering, I was greeted by the cacophony of Barney barking and loud music, a clear indication that Zoey and Barney were inside. It seemed Zoey realized I was there and promptly turned off the music.

"Mom, you're home early."

"I'm just stopping by. We've had a development." I chose not to divulge everything but did share that Kay had been abducted. There wasn't much I could do until we learned about the drivers of the vehicles that may have been involved in Kay's disappearance.

Running the plates shouldn't take too long, and between Vincent and CoCo County, it was a race of who could be faster. Technically, it was now a police matter, but it was my client and my case I brought to them. Hirsch told me he'd keep me apprised of each move in the police and FBI's tactics since we were working together.

At that point, I was supposed to be waiting to hear if the kidnappers would contact me or any of her friends, like Becky.

The police had finished their search of the apartment building and had found her cell phone tossed in the parking lot —likely thrown out the window once they got her inside the vehicle, based on the scrapes and location of where it was found.

Being on the sidelines was frustrating. Other than the search teams scouring the apartment and checking back at the Griffin house to ensure whoever took her hadn't taken her back there, there wasn't much I or anyone else could do.

Until I received the call about where to find her, I was staying put, ensuring Zoey and Barney were safe, too. What if the kidnappers came by the house? Before he was arrested, Jacob Hauser, or "Joe", may have told his associates where I lived and where they could go if they wanted to retaliate. It was unlikely, but it wasn't out of the question.

"That's awful, Mom. I can't believe it. I hope she's okay."

"So do I."

The only silver lining was that Kay had been missing only a few hours, and we knew within an hour. Thankfully, Becky had the sense to call me right away when she feared the worst.

Additionally, the workplace had surveillance video, and Vincent was quick to navigate through the back channels. However, we had to collaborate with CoCo County to ensure whoever had her would be found and that we could legally obtain a search warrant, or an arrest warrant, to bring those responsible to justice.

"How was your day, honey?" I asked, trying to bring some normalcy to our conversation.

"It's been fine. Kaylie came over for a bit, and I'm gonna see if she wants to come over tonight, too. But maybe it's not a good time?"

"It's probably best she doesn't. Maybe you should go over

there?" I suggested, voicing the thought I had been harboring. "I would feel safer if you were at Kaylie's or over at Grandma's."

Given the current circumstances, with someone targeting Kay and knowing where we lived, the risk of Zoey becoming a target to leverage against me was a genuine concern. It wasn't the first time my family and I had been in danger due to my line of work.

Although it seemed like a long shot, there was no reason to take unnecessary risks, especially when we had the support of my mom or Kaylie's family to ensure my daughter's safety.

"I can call Kaylie and see if I can stay there. Her family knows how to protect us, and they have security, too."

That Kaylie's family had security measures in place didn't surprise me. Kaylie's older sister had been kidnapped several years ago, and the family had been exceedingly vigilant about safety ever since.

"Great, I can drive you over there," I said, relieved at her willingness to stay somewhere safe.

Kaylie's house wasn't far, and under normal circumstances, she could have walked. But with dangerous individuals on the loose—individuals who had taken Kay—it was too risky, especially given what we had learned about a network of criminals from the information on the computer. These people would go to great lengths to keep their secrets and criminal activities concealed.

"Should I pack a bag?" Zoey asked.

"Yeah, maybe just an overnight bag. You never know how these things will go."

"OK, I'll call Kaylie now," she said.

As we settled on the plan, I walked into the living room, plopped down on the couch, and Barney hopped up to keep me company. It had been a while since we'd been involved in a case this dangerous, and I couldn't say I was pleased to confront another, especially with my daughter's safety at stake.

As my phone vibrated, I hoped it was Vincent or Hirsch with news about locating Kay or identifying the owners of the three potential getaway vehicles. Instead, it was Charlie.

"Hello," I answered, trying to mask the tension in my voice.

"I was just calling to see how you're doing and if you wanted to grab dinner later," he said.

Since our last date had ended rather abruptly, we hadn't seen each other, but we stayed in touch through texts and calls. I wanted to see him, but the timing was bad given the circumstances. Diving back into the dating world amidst a dangerous job and an even more perilous case was uncharted territory for both of us. "My case is heating up. I could be called away at any moment. I'm just home making sure Zoey has somewhere safe to go. She's going to a friend's for the night."

"OK, I'll be praying for you. Let me know if there's anything I can do," he offered.

"Thank you. I appreciate it."

"All right, I'll talk to you soon. I love you."

"I love you too." Feeling a little lighter, I ended the call.

Looking up, I saw Zoey standing there, jaw practically on the floor. "Did I just hear a serious set of three little words?" she asked, incredulous.

"Yes, you did," I said with a smile.

"And that's why the red roses?"

I nodded. "It's official. We're boyfriend and girlfriend."

Zoey squealed with delight and hugged me. "I'm so happy for you, Mom."

Her happiness for me was everything. I hadn't known if I would ever find love again, but I had always hoped if I did, Zoey would be happy about it too.

"Thank you, honey."

She took the seat next to me.

"Did you get a hold of Kaylie?"

"Yep. We're all set."

"Are they aware of the situation?" I shifted the topic back to safety concerns, not wanting to get too distracted by my love life. *I have a love life.*

"I explained it's a serious situation and we need to be vigilant, but we can still watch movies and eat junk food."

"Good."

"Are you going back to work after you drop me off?"

"I am."

"You heading to the station or the office?"

"Not entirely sure yet. I need to check in with Hirsch and see where the sheriff's department is at with locating Kay and the drivers of the vehicles that may have taken her."

"OK, let me pack my bag," she said as she headed to her room.

As Zoey packed, I reflected on how grateful I was for the support system around us. Indeed, it takes a village, especially when you're in a dangerous job and have people you deeply care about.

My phone vibrated again. I answered, hoping for a breakthrough. "What's up?"

"OK, I did some digging quickly. Don't tell Hirsch," he said, a mischievous tone lacing his voice. "But of the three vehicles we've identified, we've got three registered owners. The minivan is registered to a woman who, from what I can tell, has multiple children—not like our kidnapper profile. The second, a truck, belongs to an older man in his 60s—possible. But the van, registered to a Richard Cohen, is likely our guy."

"Why do you say that?"

"Because he's on the sex offender registry."

"Well done, Vincent. How did you find that out so quickly?"

"Sneaky friends, plus a couple of folks at the office. We divided and conquered. We ran backgrounds on each of the registered owners to see who would have been most likely to have taken Kay," Vincent explained with a hint of pride in his voice.

"Nicely done. You've got Cohen's address?"

"As a matter of fact, I do."

"Well done." My voice was firm. "Text it to me and I'll meet you there."

46

MARTINA

ON THE DRIVE over to Cohen's address, I briefed Hirsch on the situation and the findings that led us to the suspect's address. He acknowledged the value of the information but cautioned about the limitations we faced without a proper warrant. He said, "That's a big help to find Kay, but know that once we arrive at the suspect's house, we don't have anything usable for a warrant to arrest him or to search the house. Everything that Vincent found is good information, but it's going to take us some time to catch up and get a warrant," Hirsch explained, highlighting the frustrating bureaucratic hurdles of law enforcement.

I understood the need for procedures to protect the innocent from harassment or wrongful search and seizure, but the urgency of the situation made me anxious. "How long do you think it'll take you?"

"I've got the team working on it now. Based on the information you've given me, I could probably get a warrant in 30 minutes, maybe less if we're really fast. Just need to find a judge."

"I'll meet you at the address. Hopefully, we can get a warrant in time."

"All right, see you then. Martina, be safe. Wait for Vincent."

"I will." The call ended, reinforcing my commitment to safety—not just because I promised Hirsch, but because I was acutely aware that no case was worth risking our lives.

Prepared for what might come, I had my bulletproof vest in the trunk, alongside two firearms. Heading into a potentially dangerous situation required readiness, but Vincent and I had an advantage—they wouldn't see us coming. Vincent, who joined our firm, Drakos Monroe, a few years back, brought with him extensive weapons and hand-to-hand combat training—a requirement for all our investigators. This training made us not only tough but prepared for all situations, enabling us to perform our jobs to the best of our ability.

The suspect's address was only a ten-minute drive away—a fact that was both good and bad. It meant the suspect lived uncomfortably close, yet, looking at the registry, it was a stark reminder that potential threats could be found nearly every-where. Vigilance was crucial, *always*.

I opted to drive past the suspect's address and park a little farther down the road, planning to approach on foot. This approach allowed me time to suit up and prepare for whatever we might encounter. Hirsch, understanding the stakes, promised backup ahead of the warrant, just in case. I told him we'd be fine, but he knew better than to take chances with our safety. I didn't argue against the additional support.

I climbed out of the car and took a moment to survey the neighborhood. It was your typical suburban scene: small to moderately sized homes and a mix of older and newer vehicles parked along the streets. This wasn't the kind of place where you'd expect to find a kidnapper or a predator, but I knew all too well that monsters could be anywhere, blending in, looking just like anyone else.

I spotted Vincent's dark SUV as he pulled up behind me. Waving to him, I popped the trunk and pulled out my bullet-proof vest. Slipping it on over my T-shirt, I adjusted the straps before holstering my weapons.

He climbed out of the car, and I briefed him, "Hey, you set up?"

"Yes, ma'am," he replied with a tap on his chest.

"Hirsch said he's gonna have a couple black-and-whites in the area in case we run into any trouble, but he won't have a warrant for probably another 15 to 20 minutes."

"Kay might not have another 15 or 20 minutes."

"Exactly, and that's where we come in."

Suited up, we walked down the sidewalk toward the suspect's house. It was a quiet neighborhood where any loud sound—gunshots, screaming—would undoubtedly draw attention and likely prompt someone to call the police.

Approaching the house, I walked up the steps and knocked on the door, then stepped back. Vincent moved to the right, peering inside through the windows. No lights were on inside, suggesting that nobody was home, or that was what they wanted us to think.

"I'll check the back," Vincent whispered after a moment of silence following my second knock.

"Do you want me to go with you?" I asked, ready to back him up.

"We need a lookout."

"All right. Holler if you need me. Otherwise, I'll keep watch for the cops. I'll text you if they show up."

"You got it," he responded, and with a nod, he jogged around to the back of the house.

Standing there, on the lookout, I knew we were operating in

a gray area, pushed by urgency and a desperate hope to find Kay safe. The silent neighborhood felt like a stark contrast to the turmoil of emotions and adrenaline coursing through me. I kept a vigilant watch, ready to alert Vincent at the first sign of police arrival or any other development.

Although we maintained a cordial relationship with both the police department and the sheriff's office, we weren't exactly sanctioned to break in. The task at hand involved entering a home to search for a suspect—whom we had no official authority to question, let alone arrest. My client, Kay, was my priority, and her safety was paramount. However, if the neighbors called the police, we had no right to be there, and we could be arrested.

Thankfully, the house wasn't large, suggesting there wouldn't be too many places to hide. There was no response to my continued knocks. If nobody was home, where were Kay and Cohen?

As a police cruiser sped past, a wave of anxiety washed over me. "Shoot." *They arrived quicker than I expected.*

With a quick text to Vincent, I warned him of the police's arrival. His reply came swiftly: "Almost done."

This update was a double-edged sword. "Almost done" could mean Vincent had not found Kay, which was both a relief and a concern. If Kay wasn't there, where was she?

The sound of Vincent's footsteps hurrying along the path and the gate's metallic clink signaled his return. "All clear. There's nobody inside the house—no signs of struggle, no indications of anyone being held against their will. She's not here."

47

MARTINA

STANDING OUTSIDE COHEN'S HOUSE, Vincent and I were at a loss. The man, the van, and Kay had vanished into thin air. "We can ask Hirsch to put out an APB for Kay and Cohen and a BOLO on the license plate. Hopefully, a patrol car will spot it on the road. But if they've taken it somewhere off the beaten path, it could be parked for hours, or even days, before we find it," I said to Vincent.

Two officers approached us with smiles that seemed out of place in the current atmosphere. "Martina Monroe, Vincent Teller," one of them greeted.

"Guilty."

"I am Danbury, this is Kramer. Sergeant Hirsch said you'd be here. You're working on the case of the young woman who's gone missing," he stated, more a fact than a question.

"That's right," I confirmed, my gaze lingering on the empty house before us.

"Have you found anything?" Danbury asked.

"There's no sign of anybody in the house. We were able to see inside, but let's not delve into how," I said, sidestepping the legality of our actions for the moment.

The officers exchanged a glance. "Sergeant Hirsch said he would be here in five minutes. He wanted us to be here for backup, if needed," Kramer interjected.

"I'll give him a call," I said, already pulling out my phone.

"Yes, ma'am," came the obedient reply from Kramer.

Hirsch answered almost immediately. "What's up, Martina?"

"We're at the house, but Cohen and Kay aren't here."

"Did you look inside?" There was a hint of concern in his question.

"Off the record, yes. On the record, I don't remember," I quipped, trying to lighten the mood.

"OK, well, the warrant's not ready yet. But I'm guessing, based on the fact that he took Kay—or most likely did—we still have an open warrant to search the house. Maybe there's a computer or something that will link him to the Griffin case. I'm sure the FBI would appreciate any evidence we can find, especially if we can help decipher some of those usernames into actual persons."

"Exactly."

"Is Vincent working on the additional cameras?"

Additional cameras? I was momentarily confused. "What do you mean?"

"Well, I assume Vincent's going to pull traffic cams, following the van after he took Kay."

Had Vincent done that? I wasn't sure. "I'll have to check with Vincent; he didn't mention it. Will you put a BOLO out for the license plate of the van?"

"Yeah, it's in process right now. And an APB for Kay and Cohen. It'll go out any time now," he assured me. "I'll direct the folks here to pull footage—legally—to get us a warrant for where it ends up. It'll take some time."

"Noted."

"Are you going to stick around the scene?" he asked.

"Do you need me to?"

"Not really. If we find anything useful, we'll let you know. And of course, Jayda might come out, and we'll let the FBI know what's going on."

"Excellent. Talk to you later, partner," I said, a slight smile creeping onto my face—a smile I was guessing he could hear in my voice.

"I'll talk to you later."

I hurried back over to Vincent. "Hirsch asked if you'd pulled the traffic cams to continue following the van?"

"That's the next logical step."

"Have you already started?"

"There's no time like the present, huh? It might be tricky because each time we watch the footage, we've got to figure out where the closest camera is. It'll take a while." He hesitated for a moment, then added with a smile, "That's why I already had the team at Drakos Monroe and CoCo County get started on it."

"You're a sneaky guy, aren't you, Vincent?" I needed to remind myself to talk to Stavros about giving Vincent a raise and a promotion—he'd earned them over the last few years.

"The sneakiest," he admitted, a playful glint in his eye.

"All right. Let's get out of here. Hirsch's team will come in to search the house for any incriminating information on Cohen and the rest of the organization. Let's go back to the firm. I don't want any delays if information on Kay's location comes in."

"You got it, boss."

The team at Drakos Monroe was quick to act on getting that camera footage. They weren't technically supposed to be able to hack into the system to get it, as it was highly illegal, but desperate times called for desperate measures. If the county could find it faster than us, so be it. The urgency of our mission to find Kay and bring her home safely justified our bending of the rules, at least in our eyes. The race against time was on, and we were determined to use every resource at our disposal to ensure Kay's safety.

48

MARTINA

Vincent explained it could still be several hours before they could pinpoint where the van we thought took Kay was located. In the meantime, CoCo County was interviewing the owners of the other possible two cars that could have taken her. So far, nothing.

Waiting around doing nothing was unbearable. But our hopes were high that we'd find her. Every quiet moment I had, I prayed we'd find her safe. I couldn't help but think of her parents and the devastation they would feel if we found Kay too late and their daughter had been killed. They were so close to seeing her again; it would be cruel. Beyond cruel. Unfortunately, I knew that bad things happened to good people, and bad people, and those somewhere in between.

With my free time, I called over to Zoey to ensure they were safe and sound, and they were. From what I understood, she was cuddled up at Kaylie's house, watching movies and eating nachos. Feeling restless, I decided to check if Charlie was home. Maybe he'd want to see me, if he didn't already have plans—which I doubted since he had called earlier to see if I wanted to have dinner. It was late for dinner, but I could use something to eat, and I thought maybe he could keep me company. Sitting in my car, I called him.

"Is everything OK?" he asked.

I really needed to stop putting myself in situations where that was the first thing people asked me when they answered the phone. "Yes, I'm fine, thank you. I just... I have a couple hours while I'm waiting for information. And I was wondering, I don't know, it's late and last minute, and you've probably already had dinner..."

"Where do you want to meet, or do you want me to whip something up for you?"

My heart fluttered. "You *have* been bragging to me about what a great cook you are."

"I probably don't have time to whip up something gourmet, but I've got some chicken breast in the fridge, fixings for a salad, and I have homemade rolls in the oven."

It sounded like heaven. "Sounds great."

"You have my address. Come over anytime. I can't wait to see you."

"You too." I ended the call, started my car, and headed to Charlie's apartment.

We were so new, yet not unfamiliar, as if he had been a part of me for quite some time. He'd never cooked for me, though. It was maybe too intimate, too romantic.

After I walked the cement pathway to the front door of his apartment, I knocked. I had only been there a few times before when I picked him up to go to an event. I've never spent any time inside or at night. I kind of wondered what it would be like. Would it scream bachelor pad, with dirty floors and dishes in the sink? I knew that was a stereotype, but the thought made me cringe. There was no way Charlie was like that, though. He seemed so conscientious and put together, despite being an addict. *But you never know.*

The door opened, and his brown eyes sparkled. I could feel my cheeks warming as he said hi and leaned in for a warm, sweet kiss. "Come on in."

If I was being honest, I practically floated in, almost forgetting about the prior 12 hours—hunting bad guys and looking for those who had kidnapped Kay. He took my hand in his and said, "I'm glad you called. I was really hoping to see you."

"I wanted to see you too."

"And Zoey's OK? You said she was going to stay with a friend."

"She is. She's with her best friend, and so is Barney. I can't stay for too long, maybe just a couple of hours, but I thought I'd say hi."

He leaned in for another kiss.

I could get used to this.

I looked around the apartment, and he must've noticed because he said, "Let me show you around." He brought me into the small living room that had a sofa, coffee table, television, and not much else. The apartment appeared to be clean, like he'd vacuumed not long ago. The small dining room was connected to the living room and kitchen. The dining table had four chairs, and there was watercolor art on the walls. "That's really beautiful," I commented.

"Yeah, it's not too bad. I dabble."

A writer and a painter? "You didn't tell me that you paint."

"It's just a hobby. When I'm not writing, I like to express my creativity in other ways." He led me into the kitchen. "And this is where I make my gourmet meals, but unfortunately, not tonight. The chicken should be ready in a few minutes, and the rolls are fresh out of the oven."

I inhaled and could smell them. "Sourdough?"

"I make my own starter."

I didn't know what that meant, but it sounded impressive.

He led me down the hallway, bathroom on the left and bedroom on the right, and one more room on the left. "That's for Selena if she ever tries to contact me," he said, rather sadly.

"Still no luck?"

He shook his head. "I get it. She's a teenager, and she's probably really mad at me for leaving when I did. It was the drugs, but I wish she'd call me back."

"You know, finding people is what I do for a living. If you want me to get in contact with her for you..." I'd offered before, but still, he shook his head.

"I don't want to freak her out. I want her to come to me when she's ready."

I respected that, though I thought it was a little strange that his daughter had never returned his call. "Are you sure you have the right number for her?"

He nodded. "I do. Her name's on the voicemail." He let out a breath and said, "Can I get you something to drink? Maybe some water or iced tea?"

"I'd love an iced tea. Thank you."

He led me to a stool at the counter. "Have a seat."

I watched his every move as he leaned into the refrigerator, pulling out a pitcher of iced tea. Then I observed the silhouette of his muscles as he reached into a cupboard for a glass, set it down, and then grabbed another. If we weren't both in recovery, he might have poured wine. He knew my drink of choice was iced tea or water. It was something we shared in common, in addition to having teenage daughters and battling addiction. He poured the tea and set it down in front of me. Taking a sip, I couldn't help but watch his lips as they moved.

A timer went off, and he said, "That's the chicken." He went over to retrieve the chicken from the oven and set it down on the range. Then, he went back to the refrigerator and pulled out a bowl that held a prepared salad and a bottle of vinaigrette dressing. "I'll let the chicken rest for a few minutes. I put a light seasoning of olive oil, rosemary, and garlic on it. That OK?"

"That sounds great." I hesitated, realizing now that I'd be eating alone in front of him.

He seemed to sense my unease and said, "Don't worry, I plan to down at least one or two of those rolls. Want some butter with that?"

"Sure." Hot homemade rolls fresh from the oven with butter —my goodness.

He pulled the butter from the fridge, brought it over to the stool next to me at the counter, and presented a dish with hot rolls. The butter melted as he slathered it on. He handed me one, and the first bite was the best thing I'd eaten in years. I didn't know how I got as lucky as I did; he really seemed too good to be true.

We ate and talked. He was interested in the investigation I was working on, and he told me about his next book idea. It felt comfortable and right.

When my cell phone buzzed on the counter, I realized that three hours had passed. In that time, I had been mesmerized by Charlie and his stories. "I have to get that," I said.

He nodded with an understanding expression. "Of course."

"Vincent, what did you find?"

"I just got off the phone with Hirsch. They finished interviewing the other two potential suspects. And we're pretty certain we got it right the first time. Cohen took her. And I have a location. I'll text you the address. Our team is on the way. Where are you?"

I glanced over at Charlie. "I'm not far from there, maybe 15 minutes."

"All right, I'll see you in 15 minutes."

"Thanks, Vincent." I stood up and turned to Charlie. "I have to go. They think they found Kay's location."

"Of course, go," he said.

I paused, gave him a quick kiss, then hurried out of the apartment.

As I rushed to my car, I tried to shake off thoughts of Charlie so I could focus on Kay. Good things like me finding love again and a man like Charlie reminded me there were wonderful things in this world. And those wonderful things included finding Kay, safe and sound.

49

MARTINA

When I arrived a block away from the address of a warehouse in downtown Concord, there were at least a half dozen police cars, as well as Hirsch and Vincent. I parked my car and jogged toward where Hirsch stood with a group of uniformed officers.

"Hey. What do we have here, Hirsch?"

"We have a search warrant for the building. The team is about to go in."

"OK, I'm ready."

"What do you mean? Martina, you and Vincent aren't going in."

The confusion must have shown on my face.

"You're not with CoCo County right now. I'm sorry, Martina, I can't let you in there. If we had a contract, it'd be different. I'm sorry, we can't have a civilian in there. And quite frankly, it's not safe. It's better to have SWAT go in."

My best pal, a stickler for the rules. Maybe that was why we complemented each other. Vincent and I conceded. I hated being sidelined, but at least we'd worked together to get to this point, and I prayed Kay was inside, unharmed.

"Fine. What do you know? Have you approached the building at all?"

"We've got a tactical team surrounding the building. Whoever's in there, we've got them covered."

I looked to the side and realized there was an entire SWAT team surrounding the building already. "Good. We don't want to make the perps nervous and have them get rid of any evidence." *Including Kay.*

"No, we don't. We've got the schematics of the building from the city. We found a way to get in without alerting them. We're not knocking; we're going in, and we're going to get Kay. The team will communicate with me on my radio. They'll apprise me of the situation as they can."

Smart.

He continued, "Whoever took her isn't going to get away with it. From this moment forward, it's all by the book," he said sternly, but then softened. "And many thanks to Vincent and your team. Not saying that publicly, but thank you. We're gonna get her, Martina."

We'd better.

"OK, so when are they going in?"

He lifted his wrist. "They'll let me know when they're in position. Any minute now."

That silenced me.

A sound came over Hirsch's radio. "In position."

Hirsch looked at Vincent, me, and the officers. He said, "Go."

My heart pounded in anticipation. *Did we get here in time?*

50

KAY

Despite fear radiating down my body, my stomach rumbled—angry to have had nothing to eat since I'd been abducted and thrown in that van. What were they going to do with me? They had just left me in this windowless room knowing I was too terrified to move or try to escape. At least they had left a light on—I *hated* the dark.

I despised that closet from my childhood, and I was slowly beginning to hate that man who claimed to be my father too. Ansel—or whoever he was, the man who had stolen me, deprived me of a family, of a normal childhood, friends, my mom, my sister... It was when I was scared and felt alone that I thought of Sissy.

If I had been kidnapped when I was little, who was Sissy? She must've been Ansel's real daughter or another little girl who had been taken from her family. I just remembered being so comforted by her presence, and then devastated when she went away.

Sitting in this uncomfortable chair, I was afraid to stand up, to walk around, to do anything. Maybe I was being foolish. Maybe they had left? But I knew that wasn't true. I heard footsteps every once in a while, and whispered voices. I didn't know how to get out even if I wanted to; there were no windows, and I had no idea where I was or where they had taken me.

Footsteps approached and my body froze. I looked up to see a man I had never seen before. Unlike the man who took me, this man didn't wear a mask. Looking into his eyes though, I soon realized—it was him. He was the man who took me, the man who had threatened me earlier, asking about the laptop. Why had he removed his mask? Did it no longer matter I could identify him? I shuddered. *They're going to kill me.*

Like it wasn't enough that Ansel had stolen my life but now, even after he was gone, he would get me killed too.

"What are you going to do with me?"

"You're coming with me," he replied curtly.

"Where are we going?"

He smacked me across the face and commanded, "No more questions."

Despite my years of not crying in front of men, like my father—Ansel—the tears came now, freely. Everything from the last few weeks poured out of me—the heartbreak, not knowing a single member of my family, not knowing my name, who I had been, or what I could have been.

He dragged me by the arm into another room, where another man was. From the look in this new man's eyes, he wasn't a friend. "Who are you?" But as the words left my mouth, I knew I would regret it, as my abductor hit me again.

"Careful. She's got a pretty face," the new man warned.

A shiver went down my spine, and I knew this was going to get a lot worse before it was over.

This new man, tall and thin and wiry with gray hair, came over and stroked my hair as though I was a dog or a doll. I couldn't help but recoil.

"Don't worry, honey. We'll have so much fun together.

You're gonna love it, I promise," he said, his voice dripping with sickening sweetness.

My body jerked away but didn't get far as my abductor held me in place.

Footsteps from overhead made the wiry man step back. "Did you hear that?"

"Yeah, what was it?"

Their distraction provided a momentary relief, as my abductor released his grip on me.

"I don't know. Are you expecting anyone?" the wiry freak asked.

He shook his head.

Had Martina found me, or was it more of these creeps?

What would they do to me if I screamed? I didn't know, but I had to take that chance in case it was people looking for me.

After a deep breath, I screamed at the top of my lungs for what felt like less than a second before the man clamped his hand over my face and slammed me onto the ground.

My vision blurred, and my head pounded.

The noises above got louder and louder.

The wiry man said, "Check and see who that is; they might've heard her."

The pounding overhead was coming quicker, like footsteps on concrete, and then there was commotion and yelling.

The man released me as he ran, but men in black uniforms with big guns caught up to him and tackled him to the ground.

Another man knelt down next to me. His vest had SWAT across the front. He reached out his hand. "We're here to help," he assured.

He helped me to my feet, and I walked out of the building into the air for the first time since my abduction. The man gave me a moment before walking me down the street, and then I saw it—a bunch of police cars and two men and a woman in regular clothes. It was Vincent, Sergeant Hirsch, and Martina. Martina ran over and wrapped her arms around me as I cried. She kept saying, "You're safe now, you're safe now."

Was I really safe, or was I just safe until the next group of monsters came for me? I dared to hope that maybe, just maybe, this nightmare was finally over.

51

MARTINA

While the medics looked over Kay, I took a moment to silently thank the Lord we found her safe. But until I received news from the FBI, Jayda's team, and Hirsch confirming that anyone else who could be after Kay was no longer a threat, I wouldn't let her out of my sight. Perhaps with her rescue and the arrest of three members of that criminal organization—or so we thought—they'd understand the police were on to them and leave Kay alone.

The best we could hope for was that the FBI would take down all the members of the organization, however many there were. It was suspected that there were only a handful who were actually part of the business side of things, but there were thousands of purchasers of the heinous materials, which was disgusting to think about. The FBI was focusing their attention on all the members of the criminal organization who were procuring the images and selling them, as opposed to those who were buying them. Apparently they already had a team on that side of things.

All things considered, Kay wasn't too banged up from what I could see. It looked like they'd hit her a few times, but it was too early to tell. I didn't want to question her about it yet. She had been through so much over the last few weeks, not to mention her early years. It made me sick that other humans would do this to their fellow human beings, to children, to the innocent. Moments like these made me question God's plan. Why would He create people who would do such things to our children? I didn't understand it, and maybe I never would. But I believed in free will and that free will was what led those monsters to act as they did. I had to believe that to keep my faith, not only in the Lord but in humanity. My thoughts shifted to my daughter. I pulled out my phone and called.

"Hi, Mom, is everything OK?"

"Yes, everything's good. We found Kay, and she's OK."

"That's great to hear. Did you get the guy who took her?"

"We have them."

"Can I go home now? I mean, not that I want to." She kind of chuckled. I could hear Kaylie in the background.

"No, stay there tonight, or I can come by once I'm done. But I'd prefer you be with other people right now. We're not entirely sure where we're at with the entire lot of bad guys."

"OK, Mom. Stay safe and tell Kay I said hi and that I'm so glad she's OK."

"I will, sweetheart."

I ended the call and realized there was one more person I should call, someone who was likely waiting, just like all of us had been, for the discovery of Kay's location and her status. With a quick press of a button, I heard the recipient. "Detective Prime."

"Detective, this is Martina Monroe."

"Did you find Kay?"

"We did. She's safe. We got her."

"Oh, thank the Lord. Who was it who took her?"

"We suspect he's part of the criminal organization that her

abductor was part of. The FBI is involved, as is the local sheriff. We'll get all these guys. It may not be tonight, but at least Kay is safe. She's currently with the medical team being assessed."

"Thank goodness. I haven't left my desk—just waiting for your call."

I was really glad I called him. "As soon as she seems like she's OK to talk about her birth parents, I will, and I'll let you know what's next for their reunion."

"Thank you, Martina. I'll be waiting for your call."

I could sense his relief at the news. People didn't understand how invested some members of law enforcement could be in cases like these. There were some cases that never left you, some you never stopped investigating. I started my job as an investigator as a career option, a choice. It didn't take long to realize it was a calling, what I was meant to do—to bring answers, to find the missing, to reunite families.

Hirsch's approach interrupted my thoughts. "The medic says she looks good. She's banged up a little bit, but she said it happened recently. Sounds like we got there just in time. She was about to be handed off to a real bad guy, if you know what I mean."

"Good thing we got here when we did."

He nodded. "She's asking for you."

"Thanks."

He smiled and patted my shoulder. As I approached Kay, she gave me a smile. "Part of me knew you'd find me."

"I wouldn't have stopped looking until I had."

And to Vincent, who was standing a few steps behind me, she said, "Thank you both. If you had told me all this would've happened a month ago, I would've said you were crazy. I can't believe it all."

"How are you doing? I know it's been a traumatic time, and this didn't help."

"You know, I think I'm gonna be OK. I heard the steps above where they were holding me, and I knew I had to scream. I think it was the first time I realized I had to save myself."

Vincent and I exchanged glances, and I said, "We're glad you're safe. We did receive some news. Are you up for that?"

She nodded. "While I was in that room, alone, I had a lot of time to think. I'm ready."

I said, "Your DNA was a match for Kaitlyn Ramsey."

"I'm Kaitlyn Ramsey?" she said through tears.

"Yes."

"I figured, based on the photo, but to hear it...it feels right."

"I've spoken with a police officer, a detective in Oregon assigned to your case, and have contacted your biological parents. We spoke with them earlier. We told them about you, and they would very much like to see you. They're willing to come down to California. They understand that you may not remember them, and they're willing to respect any boundaries that you have. Take all the time you need to decide if you want to meet them, and when, and how, and where."

She sniffled, looked aside, then back at me. "I'm ready. I want to meet them. I had a lot of time to think about it when I was in there, after they took me, and I'm ready. I'm ready to meet them."

"I offered to let them come to my house to meet you there. I still think it's best you stay with me until we get the all-clear from the FBI."

She nodded. "I'd like that."

"I'll let the detective know right away, and I can call Becky —she's very worried. She's the one who alerted me that something was wrong. Do you want to call her, or do you want me to call her and let her know you're safe?"

"I'd like to talk to her. Can I borrow your phone?"

"Of course." I handed her my phone, and I watched as she

called her best friend, her chosen family when she didn't have any she knew of. I was happy for Kay and for her parents, and that she was safe.

But there was still a niggling feeling inside of me. I hadn't done my job; I hadn't found Sissy. And maybe that seemed small in that moment, considering I found something much bigger—Kay's true identity, her biological parents, the truth about her life.

But I couldn't stop looking. I didn't have much to go on, but I could pull missing person's records from the time Kay thought Sissy had died and continue looking for Cecilia Michels, the biological daughter of Sidney, because that was most likely Sissy. Kay deserved to know the truth.

52

MARTINA

In the two days since Kay's rescue, I hadn't left Kay and Zoey alone—not even to go into the office. I meant what I said—I wasn't going to let her out of my sight until I knew she was safe. Her parents were flying down later in the day for the big reunion and emotions were running high all around.

I was one of the fortunate people who had witnessed more than one reunion in my life. A reunion that wasn't statistically probable, but it wasn't a zero chance either. *There's always hope until there isn't.* Reunions were emotional, not just for those being reunited but for the bystanders as well. It was hard not to be invested in doing a job like this, especially when missing persons or murder victims were involved. There was so much heartbreak in our world; it felt good to see some of those hearts begin to mend.

"You know, Mom, if you need to go into the office, we could always go over to Kaylie's. Her mom said it was fine if Kay wanted to come over too."

"I appreciate that, but things are tense right now. We're supposed to be hearing from the FBI today. There is a lot going on."

"Is it weird that you're not part of it?" Zoey asked.

My child knew me too well. "It's difficult to not be right in it, and as you may know, I'm not always the most patient."

Zoey snorted at my admission.

I added, "But I know it's in good hands, and my job right now is to protect Kay and you, so I'm not completely sidelined. I don't always need to be going after the bad guys. Protecting the innocent, making sure the world is a safer place, is enough for me."

"How long have you been doing this job, Martina?" Kay asked.

"I'm close to nineteen years now as an investigator, nearly ten working with CoCo County off and on."

"So, finding criminals like this—it's not that unusual for you?"

"No, it's not. But it's easy to keep going when we find the truth, bring justice, and reunite families. How are you feeling about meeting your biological parents and your brother?" I turned the conversation toward her, noting her emotional state.

Her eyes lit up. *A good sign.* "I'm really excited. I'm kind of nervous, and I don't know... Is it weird to say I hope they like me?" she confided, vulnerability peeking through her excitement.

Zoey said with a supportive smile, "I'm sure they will. I mean, I haven't known you that long, but you seem pretty awesome."

I winked at my daughter and then said, "It's not uncommon, but like Zoey said, I don't think that's going to be a problem. And I've spoken with Mr. and Mrs. Ramsey and your brother Keith. They're so happy to see you. As you know, they never gave up. You've always been in their hearts and believed you would be reunited one day."

After I brought Kay home, after she was medically cleared and had finished all the questioning at the police station and with the FBI, I had explained everything to her. The conversation I had with her parents, Detective Prime, and the Facebook page dedicated to finding her. Since we'd all been staying inside over the last couple days, Becky came to visit as well, bringing her famous homemade fudge.

Becky was a good friend and I thought she would want to be there for Kay as she continued to adapt to her new reality, like meeting her family. "Are you sure you don't want Becky to be here this afternoon?" I asked.

"I think it's something I need do on my own. I mean, you will be here, but I feel like I've leaned on my friends for so long, not having a real family. I want the chance to get to know them first. Is that selfish?"

I shook my head. "Not at all. This is a big day for you."

My cell phone vibrated next to my plate of half-eaten eggs. "That's Hirsch." I excused myself from the table and said, "Hirsch, what's going on?"

"Martina, how's Kay holding up?"

"She's strong. She's doing well and is looking forward to meeting her family."

"That's great. I got a call from the FBI. They have an update for us."

"What time?"

"In about an hour. Can you come down here?"

I looked over at the kitchen and said, "Sure, but I want to bring Zoey and Kay with me. They can wait in the kitchen or a conference room. Is that OK?"

"Fine by me, but you can just call in too, if you prefer."

"No, I'll be there. We're just finishing up breakfast, and then we'll head over."

"See you soon."

With a small prayer, I hoped the FBI had good news for us, for Kay's sake.

53

MARTINA

Hɪʀsᴄʜ ᴀɴᴅ Vɪɴᴄᴇɴᴛ were waiting at the entrance as Kay, Zoey, and I arrived at the sheriff's station. Hirsch and I hugged, followed by Vincent and Hirsch exchanging handshakes with Kay, who looked apprehensive but grateful, too. She had a light in her eyes she didn't have when she first walked into my office four weeks ago. She had changed. Part of me thought it might be for the better—learning who she was, and starting to think about who she could be in the future.

Vincent eyed me and then Zoey. Amidst all the excitement, I didn't think Vincent had told anybody else about Amanda and his big news. I wouldn't be the one to share it. That was for Vincent to do.

"We've got a conference room set up for you. We've got snacks, sodas, anything you need in the kitchen. We will be just down the hall." Hirsch said as we walked back into the office area.

Heads turned as we passed, most recognizing Kay as the woman who had gone missing and been rescued. It was a win for everyone at the sheriff's department and for Drakos Monroe.

To find a kidnapped person was a feeling I could never fully put into words. Such big feelings, they could hardly be contained. Kay's cheeks turned pink, likely embarrassed by the attention.

Hirsch stopped in front of a small conference room and said, "Chairs aren't the greatest, but you can hang out in here and we'll be two doors down." He pointed to one of the larger conference rooms. "If you need anything at all, just come and knock on the door. It's okay, I promise."

Kay said, "Thank you, Sergeant Hirsch."

Jayda walked up and I waved. Jayda shook Kay's hand. "Good to see you," she said with a knowing smile that perhaps she and the FBI would have good news for us. She looked over at Zoey. "Good to see you too, Zoey." They hugged briefly before Jayda said, "Anything that makes you feel weird, anything at all seems wrong, just knock on the door and we'll drop everything to help. We'll be on a call with the FBI, but they'll understand. It's fine, but we gotta go, folks."

Hirsch said, "We'll be there in a few seconds, Jayda."

She nodded and hurried back to the conference room.

"Zoey, you know where the kitchen is. Help yourself to anything there is."

"Thanks, Uncle August."

With that, we headed toward the conference room, like in the old days of going back to the Cold Case Squad room. I guess it just went to show, whether or not we were contracted employees of the CoCo County Sheriff's Department, as long as there was a case to solve in CoCo County, our paths would cross. That, I was sure of.

We took our seats around the table, waved to Ross, and Jayda said, "Without further ado." She dialed in on the Polycom to the FBI cybercrime task force.

"Hi there, CoCo County," emanated from the speaker.

"Hey, we've got Martina, Vincent, Ross, Hirsch, and me. Who've you got?"

As the call continued, the room was filled with the voices of those on the line. "We actually have quite a few folks, but leading the discussion is Special Agent Hammer and me, Special Agent Founders, leading the task force. I've got some members of my team here—Wilton, Keegan, Bloom, and Davidson. Thought it would be good for them to hear how multi-jurisdictions can work together. We've got PIs, the sheriff's department, and the FBI all working together. This is a celebratory moment, folks." The tone was hopeful, suggesting a significant breakthrough.

Jayda, ever the one for cutting to the chase, asked, "What did you find?"

"Well, as you know we had Hauser in custody, who's not talking, but we matched his arm tattoo to that of one of the men in the videos. That plus the trespassing at the Monroe residence and his connection to the organization means he's never getting out of jail. The two suspects picked up at the scene—Roddy and Fin—didn't want to talk to us either. But considering we caught them red-handed with Kay, and the surveillance of her abduction—let's just say jail is their new home. And our pal, Ansel Griffin a.k.a. Sidney Thomas, if he were alive, he'd be their neighbor on the cell block. Based on the computer files and additional evidence collected at his house—we found a hidey-hole that had his camera equipment and photographs, likely early ones before the digital age—he was guilty as sin."

A bit of new information, but we already knew those three were busted. What about the rest of the organization?

"And?" Jayda said impatiently, a sentiment I shared. Was Kay safe? Were these criminals behind bars?

"In addition to those charges, all three are implicated in the organized crime syndicate based on a search of their computers.

We were able to match up digital footprints. We were able to use those crumbs to apprehend the other five members of the organization. The organization consisted of ten, including Ansel, who were actively procuring and selling materials. They're all in federal custody. Some are going to trial, others are negotiating deals."

The room fell silent. It seemed like the moment to cheer, but before anyone could, I needed to know definitively. "Does that mean Kay is safe?"

"She's safe. What we learned from these guys is that they just wanted the computer; they're not interested in any kind of retaliation. Kay is safe; she should be OK to go home. I know she's been staying with you, Martina."

"That's excellent news. She's also meeting her biological parents for the first time in 21 years this afternoon."

"And this is when we celebrate. These guys aren't getting out anytime soon. Most of them are on the older side, so they aren't likely to outlive their prison sentences. We'll make sure of it."

Vincent let out a, "Woo hoo!"

Smiles and hoots followed. When the room quieted, I said, "Thank you all. Take care."

Agent Founders said, "It's been a pleasure."

Looking around the room, I couldn't help but think this was not just the end of the case but perhaps the start of a new era.

When the people in this room started working together, nearly ten years ago, most of us were different people. I was a recovering alcoholic, newly sober, a single mom. Hirsch was newly divorced, swearing off children and family. Vincent was young and cocky.

Now, I'd found a new love, my daughter was in college, and I hadn't touched booze since I earned my first chip. Hirsch was married with a daughter. Vincent was married and with a baby on the way. Jayda and Ross were the constants, the ones who propped us up, knowing we needed it even when we didn't realize it ourselves. I was glad that our paths would continue to cross as long as we were in this line of work, and even if we weren't, we'd become a family, so we'd always be in each other's lives.

54

KAY

I PACED NERVOUSLY, my thoughts a whirlwind of emotions and what-ifs, while Martina and Zoey busied themselves in the kitchen, preparing for the guests who were about to change my life.

I played absentmindedly with Barney, the family's sweetheart of a dog, while my mind was consumed with the impending reunion. The idea of meeting my family—my parents and brother, the family I couldn't remember—was overwhelming.

Despite having seen their photographs and trying desperately to dredge up memories from my first four years, I failed. I also struggled with the realization that there were people out there, my real family, who had been looking for me all this time. Part of me was surprised and a little sad my real family didn't include Sissy. I knew it was likely she was Ansel's biological daughter, but I wished that was wrong and Sissy was my sister.

Martina had promised to keep looking for Ansel's second wife and his daughter, Cecilia, hoping she might be Sissy. I hoped for this too but now understood the emptiness was about more than just Sissy. Speaking with a counselor helped me realize Sissy was likely how I had coped during those initial years with Ansel, providing comfort and companionship, essential to my survival. I wished I could thank Sissy and tell her how much she meant to me, if she was still out there. I prayed she was.

Appreciative of Martina's determination, I trusted that she wouldn't rest until she had answers about Ansel's wives and daughter, and I looked forward to the day those answers would come.

As I entered the living room, Martina asked, "Can I get you anything, Kay?" Nerves made it impossible to even consider eating or drinking, but I noted Martina's concern, her repeated inquiries if I needed anything.

I didn't know what the future held with my biological family. Would we need time to get to know each other? Would I visit them in Oregon, or would they keep visiting me in California? How would it all feel? Would it be too strange, requiring even more time before I would be ready to see them again?

Then, a knock on the door broke my train of thought, with Barney barking to announce their arrival. Visitors, whether they brought danger or not, always got a greeting from Barney. I had planned on returning to my apartment, but staying with Martina, Zoey, and Barney had been comforting. Maybe I'd get my own dog someday; they were, after all, great companions.

Martina approached the door with a sense of purpose. My stomach churned, twisted into knots of anticipation and fear. It was then that Zoey came over, her presence calming in the storm of my emotions. "It'll be OK," she assured me with confidence. "Remember, they love you and they're willing to wait for you to be ready for whatever comes next."

Her words helped my nerves, echoing the kindness I'd come to associate with both her and Martina. Grateful for her support, I reached out, taking Zoey's hand in mine. The simple act was a comfort, grounding me as the sound of voices and approaching footsteps filled the air. Zoey's grip tightened, and I appreciated it.

When Martina returned, leading my family into the living room, time seemed to slow.

My mother—her features mirroring my own in ways I'd only imagined—and my father and Keith, my brother, a teenager with the same complexion as ours. For a moment, no one spoke; the weight of years lost hung between us.

Finally, Martina broke the silence. "Karen Ramsey, Ted Ramsey, and Keith Ramsey. This is my daughter, Zoey... and this is your daughter, Kay."

At her words, tears welled in my parents' eyes, and a profound sense of belonging washed over me. For the first time in my memory, I felt an overwhelming sense of love and acceptance.

Without hesitation, Zoey led the way, her hand still in mine as she guided me forward. I embraced my mother and then my father, and my brother joined in, enveloping us in a group hug filled with tears, laughter, and relief. We stayed that way for a long time. I was too afraid to let go and lose them again. Despite my fears of not remembering them, in that moment, the connection was instant and undeniable. *This is my family*.

55

MARTINA

WIPING away the tears from witnessing one of the most beautiful reunions I had ever seen, I hugged Zoey, who had tears in her eyes too. She had never seen anything like it. She asked, "You've done this before?"

I nodded. "Several times now."

"I'm so proud of you, Mom."

"It's not just me, honey."

"It's a lot you. You're the protector, the finder of the lost. You did this. Vincent and you never gave up. Uncle August, he never gives up either. The world is better because you're here."

Zoey's words caught me off guard, starting my tears again. My girl, such a beautiful young woman inside and out. Jared would've been so proud. I liked to believe he did see her, watched over her, and knew that we created the most special person together. If he was watching, I knew he would be happy for us and all our achievements, even me finding love again.

I pulled myself together and untangled myself from my daughter. Kay and her family talked and shared details about each other. I smiled as Zoey ushered them over to the couch and offered beverages or snacks.

My phone buzzed and I stepped into the hall and answered, knowing it was the office. "Hello."

"Martina, it's Mrs. Pearson."

"Hi, Mrs. Pearson. What's up?"

"We received a phone call earlier about the press release concerning Kay being reunited with her birth parents after 21 years."

I stopped moving and asked, "What kind of phone call?"

She explained, and my mouth dropped open.

"I have a name and phone number for you to call back," Mrs. Pearson said.

After ending the call, all I could think was that it was a miracle or something incredible, akin to when the stars align to form a constellation or when we found a missing person alive after 21 years.

There was hard work involved, and there were steps to follow to get there, but it was a miracle nonetheless. There was no other way to describe it.

I took the information and promised to look into the situation. I had to make sure the person who left the message wasn't a crackpot or somebody who was intending on causing harm to Kay.

We expected a few crazies to come out of the woodwork when we, Drakos Monroe, the sheriff's department, and the FBI allowed the media to run the story. We asked them to hold off until Kay was able to meet her parents before broadcasting the news. Since Vincent had ties to the media, they agreed. But now, the story was everywhere.

A young girl was kidnapped at four years old by a man with three different aliases, who was now deceased. His associates, part of a much bigger organization of criminals, were also in federal custody and likely to be prosecuted to the full extent of the law.

Returning to the living room, I smiled out at the Ramsay family, feeling their joy and togetherness enveloping the room. Zoey sidled up next to me, curiosity painting her face. "What was that about?"

"I'm not 100% sure, but once we're finished up here, I'll call Vincent. We'll get right on it."

"Sounds ominous," Zoey said in a hushed tone.

Ignoring the comment, I looked out at the family. "Can I get you anything?"

Mrs. Ramsey said, "No, you've already done so much, Martina. I just can't believe it. Thank you so much."

The rest of the family echoed the sentiment, their gratitude filling the room. It then occurred to me that I should've invited Vincent. He had been so integral to this reunion. It was just like me to forget. "It wasn't only me, but Vincent, my associate, too."

"Oh yeah, Vincent." Kay smiled.

Mrs. Ramsey said, "We would love to meet him."

"I can give him a call. He could come over."

Kay said, "If it's no trouble."

"I'll call him." Back in the hall, I called Vincent and filled him in on the message I'd received and asked him to look into it before heading over.

As we sat and chatted for the next hour, it was heart-warming to witness how, despite the years spent apart, they were already fusing together as a family. Kay had an undeniable glow about her like she had found home.

A knock on the door came, followed by the Barney alarm. Zoey made a move to answer it, but I excused myself, saying I would see to it. I walked down the hallway and opened the door. There stood Vincent, a mischievous look on his face.

I couldn't help but ask, "What did you find out?"

"A lot," he replied, his tone serious.

As Vincent explained, chills ran down my body.

56

MARTINA

When I received the news a week before, I had a feeling it was for real, and Vincent's research proved it. The call, responding to the news coverage of Kay's discovery and reunification with her parents, did produce quite a few calls—some nasty, some encouraging, and some jerks making crazy claims. But the one that Mrs. Pearson forwarded to me wasn't any of those.

And now, Vincent and I sat in front of Lia Caldwell and her mother, Jane Caldwell, as we listened intently while they told us their story.

Jane said, "When I met Rex Michels—or I guess his real name was Sidney Thomas—he seemed really charming and kind. Swept me off my feet, really. It was a whirlwind romance. We had only been dating for about two months when he proposed. I thought I'd found the man of my dreams. But after we said, 'I do,' things changed—and changed fast. It was like getting whiplash. He'd been sweet and caring, attentive, even. But as soon as we moved in together and I had that ring on my finger, I couldn't go anywhere without his approval. He had me quit my job, saying that my job was to take care of him and the house. That wasn't what we'd talked about when we were engaged."

I nodded. "I understand." It was a classic sign of an abuser trying to control their victim in every aspect of their life, making her quit her job in order to control her comings and goings as well as her financial situation, making it difficult for her to leave him.

She continued, "I got pregnant pretty quickly, and I was so happy, even though I'd become lonely, not being able to go to work or really go anywhere, although my parents still insisted on coming by the house to check on me. They didn't like Rex, not one bit, but I was headstrong." After a pause, she smiled at Lia and continued. "After Cecilia was born, or as we now call her, Lia, his abuse got worse. He hit me. He locked me in closets, forbade me from going anywhere. And I didn't tell anyone about it, but my parents knew. They had quite a few run-ins with each other. He would argue with my parents, and of course he ended up winning—especially since I told them to leave, claiming that I was fine. I'll never forget the look in my dad's eyes when I pushed him out the last time." She paused to compose herself. "It got to the point where I couldn't even see my parents because he threatened to kill me and the baby if I did. So, I endured several years of abuse from him, all forms. I don't need to get into it," she said, as tears escaped from her eyes.

Her daughter put a hand on hers and said, "Do you want me to tell her?"

She shook her head. "I can do it. He doesn't have that power over me anymore. I'm glad he's dead," she said quietly before continuing. "My moment of realization came when I saw bruises on Lia, who was about six years old then. Bruises in areas where there shouldn't be any. That's when I knew it was either I leave, or this man kills me or does something even worse. Worse than he'd already done."

I looked over at Lia, who was holding up surprisingly well. "I asked her about it. She didn't remember anything. When I questioned him about it, I said, 'How did that happen?' He blamed it on me. He said I must've done it, that I must've been careless and hurt her somehow. That's not how things work. I wasn't that stupid." Her voice shook as she spoke.

I said, "Take your time."

She nodded.

Her voice wavered as she continued. "I got really suspicious, started searching for any kind of proof. And I found a photograph...of my little baby...with no clothes on. I confronted him with it. I screamed, yelled—that was the day he gave me the worst beating of my life. He took the photo and burned it. As soon as he went to work the next day, I called my parents, and they came and picked us up. He tried to get us back, and my father threatened him. Said if he laid a hand on either of us ever again, he would shoot him with his shotgun."

Her story was chilling. What would have happened if she hadn't had protective parents to run to?

Jane went on. "I was naïve to think that was the end of it. That he'd just let us go," she said, shaking her head. "No, he got a lawyer and demanded joint custody. He was granted joint custody, where he had visitation every other weekend. I fought him each time, begging him not to take her. My father and I tried to hide her. His response was to call the police, who had threatened to arrest me and my parents if we didn't give him Lia. But of course, once he took her and the police were gone, he threatened to kill all of us. That went on for two years."

After wiping her tears, she said, "Those were the years that Lia said she had a friend. Why don't you tell her honey?"

Lia, or rather *Dr. Lia Caldwell*, spoke up, "There was a little girl when I would visit my dad. She was younger than me by a couple of years. I remember her so vividly; she was my only friend when I was at my dad's. We would hide under the covers, sneak treats. It was because of her that I was able to get through those two years with him before we ran."

"And you believe that little girl is Kaitlyn Ramsey?"

She nodded. "When the news aired and I saw my dad's picture on the news, that he was a doctor, and that he'd abducted a little girl and they showed the photo, I knew it was her. Before that, my mom and my stepdad told me that she was an imaginary friend. Psychologists told me she was likely not real, something I had made up, a figment I created to deal with the trauma of being at my father's. But I knew she was real. Part of me always knew she was real. And so, when I graduated from medical school, I thought everything would be fine, and I'd feel whole and complete, like I had my life together. But I always thought back to her, to that little girl we called KK."

"What did she call you?" I asked.

"She called me Sissy. Dad said that she was my sister; she was so little all she could say was 'Sissy'; she couldn't say Cecilia."

I nodded, feeling a lump form in my throat as I realized I was getting choked up again.

We hadn't told Lia that one of the reasons Kay had come into our offices was, in fact, to find her. Of course, she thought Sissy was her sister who had passed away, and she was looking for her grave, not a living relative.

"I started asking my mom and my stepdad about the girl after I graduated from medical school. They still insisted that she was a figment of my imagination and that I never had a sister. So, I went to a private investigator, and because my stepdad's a US Marshal, he knew the investigator. The investigator called him and told him what I was doing. I wasn't supposed to look into our past. Mom told us that we had to run and hide from the monsters, and that we could never talk about it or go back."

The eerie similarities of Lia and Kay's experiences were unique but connected. I wondered if Kay understood that she was how Cecilia had gotten through those two years too. The two girls, although not blood-related, were bonded even all these years later. "That's incredible that you remember her."

"I don't think there's ever been a time I didn't think of her. And then, after my mom told me why we ran away from my dad, I worried that she had been a victim, and that's why I wanted to find her. When we saw Dad's face on the news, and then hers, I was in a state of disbelief and knew it was KK."

I nodded and said, "Kay was told that you were her sister and that when you were eight, you died suddenly, and her own mother—your mother, as well—died during her childbirth. She came to us to find your gravesite because she thought that her father, or who she thought was her father, would want to be buried next to you."

"Seriously?" she asked, eyes wide.

I nodded. "We looked for you. We were able to unravel all his identities, from Sidney Thomas to Rex Michels to Ansel Griffin, and we found that he'd been married a second time, had a child, but then your trail went cold after he left Oregon and moved to California. It was as if you disappeared." We had feared they were killed, buried somewhere, but there were no missing person's reports.

Jane said, "I'll take that one. When Lia was eight, I met my now-husband. He's a US Marshal, and I told him the situation, and he helped us form new identities. And so we did, and my parents too. After we acquired new identities, we moved so that he would never find us."

Vincent and I exchanged glances, understanding that it was

the only way they could've hidden from Ansel. "Why didn't you go to the police?" I asked.

"Back then, they wouldn't have believed me. We didn't have any evidence. And she didn't remember any of it."

"The FBI Cyber Crime Task Force, who took on the case, believes that the children who were abused in the videos and photographs had been drugged, and they weren't conscious during the acts."

Jane said, "That makes sense."

"Before we move on, during our research, we were able to find a marriage certificate to his first wife, Sinead. Did he ever talk about her to you?"

Her eyes widened. "Yes. He killed her."

"He told you that?" I asked.

"When we were married, he reminded me of it all the time. He said if I didn't do what he said, I'd end up just like Sinead."

"Did he ever mention where her body was buried or how he got away with it? She's currently listed as a missing person."

"He said"—she shook her head—"after he strangled her, he dismembered her body and threw it in the ocean. At the time, he lived in Washington state. He said he took a ferry with a suitcase full of her body parts and rented a boat once he was on Bainbridge Island and scattered her body." She grimaced. "He said because he was a doctor, he knew how to dismember the body pretty easily. And if I ever disobeyed him or crossed him, I'd end up just like her, and nobody would ever find me or know what happened to me. That's why we changed our identities and hid from him. I knew what he was capable of."

Jane Caldwell had been carrying a lot over the last 20-plus years. I scribbled a note to contact the Washington FBI to give them the tip.

"I'm so sorry you had to go through that, both of you."

"Thank you. Lia started counseling after she heard the

news, and I've been in counseling for a long time trying to deal with it. It's a relief he's gone, and he can never get to us," Jane said.

I straightened up. "Thank you for coming in, for calling. I know it'll mean a lot to Kay. You meant a lot to her, Lia. And she is in our conference room waiting for you."

"She's here?" Lia asked, eyes wide.

"Yes, she is. Before we could let you meet her, we had to make sure you were who you claim. As you can imagine, after the news coverage of her discovery and reunification with her family, we've gotten a lot of calls, and not all of them kind. So, we wanted to protect her. She's been through a lot over the last month."

"I can't imagine. But I can't wait to see her again."

I said, "She's with her biological parents. She wanted them to be there when she saw you again. They're grateful she had you those two years. Kay says it's because of you she was able to adjust during that time. She said she's never forgotten you."

After a few more tissues, we headed down the hall to Kay and her parents and her brother, who hadn't been separated since their meeting the previous week. The reunion, charged with emotion and the weight of years lost and found again, was a testament to the resilience of the human spirit and the unyielding bonds of love.

The sound of the knock on the door resonated in the small room, and I promptly stood, a gesture mirrored by my mother, father, and brother. The door swung open to reveal Martina, her smile broad and welcoming. "Hi," she said. "Lia is here with her mother, Jane."

And moments later, Vincent and Lia entered, trailed by a woman whose presence was commanding—her light hair and eyes surveying the room. A sense of familiarity washed over me as I realized she was the woman from the photo albums—Ansel's second wife.

Suddenly, a woman with hazel eyes and an infectious smile caught my gaze.

Our eyes locked, and I whispered, "Sissy."

As she stepped closer, she uttered, "KK."

We embraced, and the world around us faded into the background. Despite the short time together in our youth, the connection was there, as if no time had passed at all. "I'm so glad you called," I managed to say, pulling away slightly.

"Martina told me everything. I'm so sorry."

However, Martina interjected, "We haven't told you everything. Perhaps it's best if you two share your memories of each other, with each other."

Nodding, I shared with Lia the profound impact she had on my life. "Every time I felt scared, I remembered how you taught me to hide from the monsters under those covers. Your presence, your comforting whispers, and your smile and laugh have stayed with me through the years," I confessed.

Her smile broadened, tears glimmering in her eyes. "I've never stopped thinking of you either. Those two years were incredibly challenging, but knowing you saw me as your sister—despite what everyone said—helped me through. I've always thought of you as my sister, too."

It felt as though our souls were destined to cross paths during those tumultuous years. Despite the devastation, the silver lining was our meeting.

As I glanced around the room, reflecting on the recent whirlwind of revelations, my identity was clear before me. I wasn't just Kaitlyn Ramsey from Oregon; I was someone loved by a family that extended beyond conventional boundaries—I not only had a real mom and dad and a little brother, but I also had a sister.

In that moment, seeing Sissy for the first time in years and enveloped by the love of my family, I felt an overwhelming sense of freedom and completeness. It was, undoubtedly, the most profound happiness I had ever experienced.

It had made the decision to leave my job and pack up my apartment to move to Oregon to be close to them easy. Though it meant moving away from my best friend, Becky, I believed we'd visit often and always be a part of each other's lives. Becky wasn't just my best friend, but my family too. What more could I possibly ask for?

MARTINA

THANKSGIVING, THE FOLLOWING YEAR

WITH THE LAST of the dishes done, I picked up the sparkly diamond band from the dish next to the sink and slid it back onto my ring finger. As I stared down at it, disbelief washed over me. It seemed unreal that it was actually mine. A part of me had resigned to the idea that I would never get married again, let alone find the love of my life. Yet, here I was, proving myself wrong.

Charlie came up behind me, his hands finding my waist gently as he planted a soft kiss on my cheek. "I think it suits you," he murmured.

Turning to face him, I wrapped my arms around his neck and replied with a smile, "I'm beginning to understand why Zoey loves sparkles. I love it."

He smiled back, his eyes lighting up. "Well, I'm glad," he said, pulling me closer.

Our engagement happened over the summer, after a year filled with love and discovery. Charlie had been so sure, so certain that I was the one for him. I didn't hesitate for a second when he knelt down on one knee on a beach in Maui, asking me to be his wife, his partner, and best friend for the rest of our lives.

We shared a quick kiss before he whispered, "Time for dessert."

"Did you see what my mom brought?"

With a smile, he said, "Pumpkin pie, apple pie, and a pumpkin cheesecake."

"I want a piece of each."

"Me too," he said, his eyes twinkling with mischief.

Just then, Zoey walked into the kitchen. "Oh, you two are so cute," she said, her voice filled with a mix of amusement and affection.

I could feel my cheeks heating up, embarrassed. My daughter had always been a source of strength for me, and even though I felt a bit self-conscious, I hoped she learned from our love and would one day find her own love like Charlie and I shared.

She had been overjoyed upon hearing the news of our engagement, immediately asking if she could play a role in the wedding. Years ago, I had promised her that if I ever remarried, she could be in the wedding. True to my word, I asked her to be my maid of honor, standing by my side as I married Charlie.

However, we hadn't set a date yet.

My hesitation stemmed from the fact that Charlie hadn't been able to get in touch with his daughter, Selena. It didn't feel right going forward with the wedding without having met my future stepdaughter. Charlie insisted he wanted to handle the relationship with his daughter, but deep down, I felt we should find her and talk to her before tying the knot. Our future felt like it was on hold, waiting for a piece of our new family puzzle to click into place.

"I was just coming to get the pies. Ted says he was the taste-tester and they're awesome," Zoey explained as Charlie and I untangled ourselves to help her bring the desserts out to the table.

Heading toward the table, it was a heartwarming sight; everyone we cared about was gathered around the Thanksgiving table. The table was adorned with sparkly pumpkins, a touch courtesy of Zoey, alongside some green foliage my mother had brought.

Hirsch sat contently next to Kim, with Audrey occupying the seat beside him. Each day, she seemed to mirror him more and more. Next to them were Mom, Ted, and of course my brother Darren and his girlfriend who had celebrated a sober year. Vincent sat next to them, Amanda absent, likely chasing after their toddler, Caden.

Over the years, so much had changed for all of us. It felt like we had all come together at a time when we needed each other the most. Each of us, a little bit broken in our own way, were now whole and part of an incredible family, both chosen and blood, happy and healthy.

After serving the pie, we took our seats. Amanda emerged from around the corner, carrying the wriggly one-year-old Caden in her arms, his eyes wide with curiosity and a clear fascination with Barney. Amanda and Caden had snuck Barney bits of turkey earlier, which caused Caden to light up each time Barney grabbed it from his chubby little hand.

Vincent offered to take Caden so Amanda could enjoy her pie. "That's okay, you eat first. I need to tickle this little guy," she said, as Caden's giggles echoed throughout the room.

Charlie sat down next to me, and despite the warmth and joy of our gathering, I couldn't help but sense he was missing his daughter.

After we had cleaned up and our guests had departed and Zoey retired to her room to make plans with Kaylie, I sat down with Charlie on the sofa.

"How are you doing?" I asked, seeking the truth behind his smile.

He entwined his hand with mine. "I've never been happier," he said, but the hesitation in his voice was obvious.

"But?" I prompted, knowing there was more he wished to express.

"I wish she'd call me back."

The investigator in me feared there was more to his daughter's silence than teen angst. "I know you've wanted to handle it yourself, but maybe we should try to find her and talk to her in person. She should be here with us. If she sees you're in a stable relationship, and you're getting married, and you've been sober for two years... It's different this time."

Charlie conceded. "You're right. As happy as I am with you, without my daughter, I feel like part of me is missing. I want her with us."

I do too. "Then it's settled. I'll find Selena."

And I would. Because that's what I do. I seek justice, protect the innocent, find the missing, and reconnect families. Selena was family, and every part of my being told me I *needed* to find her.

THANK YOU!

Thank you so much for reading the Martina Monroe series! If you didn't know, Martina's character was first created in the Selena Bailey series. And it was while writing Selena's story that I fell in love with Martina and knew I had to write her backstory before she ever met Selena and her father Charlie. It has taken thirteen books (including the prequel, *Crashing Down*) to tell Martina's backstory and to connect her with her future husband and stepdaughter.

If you haven't read the Selena Bailey series, that is your next step in finding out what happens next for Martina and Selena (Note: The Selena Bailey series is told mostly from Selena's point of view. She is a young woman aged 17-22 who uses *stronger* language than Martina!). If you've already read Selena Bailey, or the Selena Bailey series doesn't sound right for you, not to worry, this is *not* the end. I love Martina and the gang too much to say goodbye just yet!

Martina *and* Selena will return, picking up after the end of the Selena Bailey series, in: **Her Fearless Pursuit, Martina Monroe Book 13. Release date: February 21, 2025**.

ALSO BY H.K. CHRISTIE

The Martina Monroe Series

Crashing Down

What She Left

If She Ran

All She Wanted

Why She Lied

Secrets She Kept

What She Found

How She Fell

Her Last Words

Who She Was

How She Escaped

Lies She Told

Echoes of Her

The Selena Bailey Series

A suspenseful series featuring a young Selena Bailey and her turbulent path to becoming a top notch PI - led by her mentor, Martina Monroe.

Not Like Her

One In Five

On The Rise

Go With Grace

Flawless

A Permanent Mark A heartless killer. Weeks without answers. Can she move on when a murderer walks free? If you like riveting suspense and gripping mysteries then you'll love *A Permanent Mark* - starring a grown up Selena Bailey.

The Neighbor Two Doors Down is a a dark and witty psychological thriller. If you like unpredictable twists, page-turning suspense, and unreliable narrators, then you'll love *The Neighbor Two Doors Down*.

ABOUT THE AUTHOR

H. K. Christie watched horror films far too early in life. Inspired by the likes of Stephen King, Jodi Picoult, true crime podcasts, and a vivid imagination she now writes suspenseful thrillers.

She found her passion for writing when she embarked on a one-woman habit breaking experiment. Although she didn't break her habit she did discover a love of writing and has been at it ever since.

When not working on her latest novel, H.K. Christie can be found eating & drinking with friends, walking around the lakes, or playing with her favorite furry pal.

She is a native and current resident of the San Francisco Bay Area.

To learn more about H.K. Christie and her books, or to purchase signed paperbacks and audiobooks direct from the author, or simply to say, "hello", go to **www. authorhkchristie.com**.

At **www.authorhkchristie.com** you can also sign up for the H.K. Christie reader club where you'll be the first to hear about upcoming novels, new releases, giveaways, promotions, and a free e-copy of the prequel to the Martina Monroe Thriller Series, *Crashing Down*!

ACKNOWLEDGMENTS

To Becky Sumner, I want to thank you for being a beautiful person. It is incredible how you have managed to foster such a warm and caring environment (online!) in the Book Swap Central group, and I'm grateful to have been author of the month where I was able to get to know the group and you a little better. Happy reading.

To Carol Ann Henson, Joy Lorton, and Jerilyn Schad. Not only did you win the contest to have a character named after you, or to pick a name, in this book, but you're also some of my favorite readers! Thank you!

Many thanks to my Advanced Reader and Street Teams. These wonderful readers are invaluable in taking the first look at my stories and helping find typos and spreading awareness of my stories through their reviews and kind words.

To my editor, Paula Lester, a huge thanks for your careful edit and helpful comments and proofreader Ryan Mahon for catching those last typos. To my cover designer, Odile, thank you for your guidance and talent.

To my best writing buddy, Charlie, thank you for the looks of encouragement and reminders to take breaks. If it weren't for you, I'd be in my office all day working as opposed to catering to all of your needs and wants such as snuggles, scratches, treats, and long, meandering walks. To the mister, thank you, as always, for putting up with me especially when I'm approaching one of my overly ambitious, self-imposed deadlines.

Last but not least, I'd like to thank all of my readers. It's because of you I'm able to continue writing stories.

Made in the USA
Las Vegas, NV
21 June 2024